KU-189-846

24:7

The cutting edge of
Mills & Boon® Medical Romance™

The emotion is deep
The drama is real
The intensity is fierce

24:7

Feel the heat—
every hour...every minute...every heartbeat

As a twelve-year-old **Amy Andrews** used to sneak off with her mother's romance novels and devour every page. She was the type of kid who daydreamed a lot, and carried a cast of thousands around in her head. From quite an early age she knew that it was her destiny to write. So, in between her duties as wife and mother, her paid job as Paediatric Intensive Care Nurse and her compulsive habit to volunteer, she did just that! Amy Andrews lives in Brisbane's beautiful Samford Valley with her very wonderful and patient husband, two gorgeous kids, a couple of black Labradors and six chooks.

Recent titles by the same author:

THE NURSE'S SECRET SON
EARTHQUAKE BABY
THE MIDWIFE'S MIRACLE BABY

MISSION:
MOUNTAIN RESCUE

BY
AMY ANDREWS

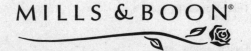

MILLS & BOON®

My thanks to Warrant Officer Class 2 Derek Davis,
Army Malarial Institute, Gallipoli Barracks, Enoggera,
for his time and expertise.

DID YOU PURCHASE THIS BOOK WITHOUT A COVER?

If you did, you should be aware it is **stolen property** as it was reported
unsold and destroyed by a retailer. Neither the author nor the publisher
has received any payment for this book.

All the characters in this book have no existence outside the imagination
of the author, and have no relation whatsoever to anyone bearing the
same name or names. They are not even distantly inspired by any
individual known or unknown to the author, and all the incidents are
pure invention.

All Rights Reserved including the right of reproduction in whole or
in part in any form. This edition is published by arrangement with
Harlequin Enterprises II B.V. The text of this publication or any part
thereof may not be reproduced or transmitted in any form or by any
means, electronic or mechanical, including photocopying, recording,
storage in an information retrieval system, or otherwise, without the
written permission of the publisher.

This book is sold subject to the condition that it shall not, by way of
trade or otherwise, be lent, resold, hired out or otherwise circulated
without the prior consent of the publisher in any form of binding or
cover other than that in which it is published and without a similar
condition including this condition being imposed on the subsequent
purchaser.

MILLS & BOON and MILLS & BOON with the Rose Device
are registered trademarks of the publisher.

First published in Great Britain 2006
Harlequin Mills & Boon Limited,
Eton House, 18-24 Paradise Road, Richmond, Surrey TW9 1SR

© Amy Andrews 2006

ISBN 0 263 84732 2

Set in Times Roman 10¼ on 12 pt.
03-0506-55655

Printed and bound in Spain
by Litografia Rosés, S.A., Barcelona

PROLOGUE

HOLLY briefly scanned the elegant room. Her eyes quickly assessing each male occupant. A glance at the creepy little man approaching fast made her search all the more desperate.

A man entered her peripheral vision and sauntered towards the bar. His short black hair, lightly streaked with grey was rumpled and his tie askew. He looked tired but there was an unmistakable air of authority about his tall erect frame. She felt a silly little flutter in the region of her heart. Richard.

'There you are, darling.' Her tone one of accusation. 'We must have had our wires crossed. I've been waiting for you in the other bar.'

A frown furrowed his forehead. Holly launched herself into his arms and he grabbed her shoulders to steady her from the clumsy impact. She pressed a kiss against his lips and he felt his surprise give way to stupor.

His lips remained immobile. He wanted them to move. After all, it had been a long time since she had kissed him with such blatant appreciation. A whole month since she had kissed him at all. And, heaven knew, he'd missed it like crazy. But he seemed to have developed a short circuit between his brain and the nerves to his face. In fact, his entire face seemed to be stricken by some weird kind of palsy.

As she released his lips, he saw disappointment and accusation in her eyes and, despite knowing how pointless it was, he wanted to rectify it immediately. It was easy to figure out what was happening. Some guy was trying to hit on her and she needed him.

'Sweetheart.' He smiled a dazzling smile and pulled her to him again, giving her the kind of kiss he should have given her before. The kind of kiss that had made their tempestuous relationship so addictive. So hard to walk away from. When he pulled away they were both slightly out of breath.

Oh, man! She had missed his kiss. Holly stared at him and he stared back, a smile touching his full lips. She felt the familiar zing between them and her gut told her it couldn't possibly be over.

Her pursuer cleared his throat and she dragged her eyes away from Richard. Time to ditch the Leech, who had suckered up to her half an hour ago and who she just couldn't shake.

'And who's this darling?'

'Oh, just some nice man who kept me company in the bar.' She could afford to be gracious now. No need to hurt the Leech's feelings altogether.

'So, you really are meeting someone?' His nasal voice crawled along her spine. 'You must be Holly's fiancé?'

'That's right,' Holly supplied, quickly squeezing Richard's hand, imploring him to play along and not blow her story. 'Richard.'

She felt his hand tense in hers, his body still, his spine straighten, and he gave her a hard look.

'Darling?' She shoved him gently with her shoulder. Do this for me, just this one thing, her eyes begged him.

'Er, hmm, yes.' He cleared his throat. 'Thanks for looking after my girl. You never know what predators are out there these days.' And then he turned them around and walked her to the bar.

Holly sat down next to him and could feel his hostility.

'Thank you, Richard. He was such a creep, he just wouldn't take the hint.'

'What are you doing here, Holly?'

Just like Richard to cut straight to the chase. 'I just wanted to say goodbye.'

'I thought we did that a month ago.'

'Please, Richard,' she pleaded. I will not cry. 'You're leaving for Africa tomorrow. Can't we at least have a farewell drink?'

Richard sighed and looked into her lovely young face and the urge to leave the bar with her right away and say good bye properly was almost overwhelming. 'Chardonnay, Pollyanna?'

Holly smiled despite the wretchedness wrought by the familiar nickname and memories of their first-ever meeting in this very bar two years before he swamped her. She had plonked herself next to him after a particularly horrible day at work and he had taken pity on her and offered to buy her a drink. She remembered it as if it had happened yesterday.

'You sure you're old enough to drink?'

'Of course.' She smiled. 'Why? How old do you think I am?'

'Twelve,' he said, sipping at the froth on his beer, not even looking at her.

She giggled. 'I'm twenty-one.'

'Egad.' He clapped his hand to his forehead theatrically. 'All grown up.'

'How old are you, then?'

'Way older than that.'

'Oh, come on, Methuselah.' She nudged his arm. 'Spill the beans.'

'I'm thirty-six.'

'Oh, no!' she gasped, mimicking him. 'Practically in your dotage.' And she giggled again. 'That's only fifteen years' difference.'

'Forget it. I'm way too old for you, babycakes.'

'Oh, pish!'

'Pish?' He shook his head. 'Your parents should have named you Polly instead of Holly. Short for Pollyanna.'

Holly laughed, finding the idea outrageously funny.

'I rest my case,' he said derisively.

They sipped at their drinks for a few moments. 'So, old man, what do you do?'

'I'm a soldier.'

She whistled. 'Impressive.'

'Pollyanna.' He rubbed his hands through his hair in exasperation. 'How do you know I didn't just tell you a big, fat lie?'

'Why would you lie?'

He shrugged. 'Get you into bed.'

She laughed again.

'You can laugh. Lots of women want to sleep with men in uniform.'

'Well, rest assured, Richard, I wouldn't sleep with you because you were a soldier.'

'Good for you.' He raised his glass to her and took a swig.

'I'd prefer to sleep with you because you're the sexiest man I've ever met.'

Richard swallowed his mouthful of beer hard and stared at her.

'Sorry.' She said, smiling, looking at his shocked face. 'Not a very Pollyanna-like thing to say, huh?'

'Not the Pollyanna I remember.'

'Fiancé?' he said after the barman had paced her drink in front of her and she had taken a sip.

Holly came back from the past. 'Fiancé's are always much more threatening than boyfriends.' And a girl could dream, right?

They drank in silence for a few minutes.

'You will be careful over there, wont you?' Holly felt nauseous every time she thought about him in the middle of a war zone.

'It's a UN humanitarian mission. It's perfectly safe.'

His dismissal of her fears were typical. In retrospect he had always treated her as a bit of a kid, dismissing her opinions and telling her only what he'd thought she'd needed to know. Holly had known for a while that she wanted more. To be treated like an equal. Like an adult. To get married and start a family.

'I've seen the television footage. It looks terrible.'

He took another mouthful of beer.

'It's not too late to back out,' Holly said softly.

'Yes, it is.' He put his glass, down and turned to her. 'And even if it wasn't, I'd still be going. This is what I do, Holly. I put on my uniform and I go where and when my country tells me. These people need us. I can help them.'

'And what about me? I need you, too.'

Richard felt her words go straight to his groin. She was incredibly appealing…too appealing. And she was also wrong. She didn't need someone fifteen years older who was married to his job. She needed someone who had a joy and zest for life to match her own. She was twenty-three for heaven's sake. She needed to get out in the world and explore it. See other countries, taste other cuisines, be with other men.

'No. You need a direction in your life, Holly. A purpose.'

'I did have a purpose in my life.' I wanted to marry you and have your babies. Was that such an awful thing?

'Other than me.'

'You know me, Richard,' she said sipping her wine, 'I've always been a little between things.'

'How nice for you,' he said, his voice laced with derision. Her easy-come, easy-go attitude had always been at complete odds to his. In fact, in some perverse kind of way it was what had intrigued him. And irritated him the most. Nice to know he and his kind would keep her world safe while she was 'between things'. 'You want something to do? There's a whole screwed-up world out there, Pollyanna. I'm sure you'll find some way to decorate it.'

His dismissal of her rankled. 'You always did think I was kind of frivolous, didn't you?'

'No, Holly,' he sighed, rubbing his fingers through his hair, messing it further. 'Look, I told you at the beginning this would never work.'

'Because of my age?'

'Yes, amongst other things. I am too old for you, Holly. We are at different stages in our lives. We're too different.'

'Would those other things have anything to do with your emotionally stunted upbringing? Or your unhealthy dependency on your job for validation of your life?' She was trying not to be bitter.

When she said it like that it made him seem so emotionless. So cold. But he had warned her he wasn't good at relationships. He'd had no yardstick in his life worth a damn.

'I've always been up front with you, Holly.'

'Please, Richard.' She faced him and placed her hand on his. 'Don't shut me out. You're going away? So go. I know I can't stop you but I can be waiting here for you when you get back.'

He looked into her earnest face and thought how much he desperately wanted to take her up on it. Having Holly to come home to would be nice. But, face it, after the initial high of frenzied sexual activity wore off they'd be back at square one. Chemistry had never been their problem. She wanted things he wasn't prepared to give. She needed to move on and he was not used to needing anyone.

He removed her hand. 'We've been through this, Holly. Don't make it harder than it is.'

Holly blinked hard and nodded. She wasn't being fair. 'Then take me home and make love to me one last time.' Holly threw away her last shred of dignity, but she needed to be held by him now more than her next breath.

Richard swallowed hard. Being with Holly one last time sounded like heaven. But he knew once he started he wouldn't want to stop, and he'd never want to get out of bed in the morning and leave.

And she'd look at him with those eyes and he'd feel terrible walking away from her. He didn't need that, going to a war zone. He figured life in general would probably be pretty crappy for the next six months, even without a guilt trip from Holly. He'd made the break. He needed to keep it clean.

'I can't, Holly.'

Of course he couldn't. Richard was an honourable man. Twenty-one years in the military had seen to that. Tears rose in her throat but she swallowed them. She'd laid herself bare enough today. She would not disgrace herself completely by sobbing over his shirt in a public bar.

He drained his beer glass and pushed himself off the stool. 'Goodbye, Holly. Take care.'

'Wait,' she said, whipping the pen out of his shirt pocket and desperately scribbling on a bar napkin. 'It's my new number. Call me when you get back.'

'No.'

'Please?' she asked, returning his pen to his pocket along with the napkin.

'It's over, Holly.' He reached into his pocket, his fingers stilling as she placed her hand on his.

'Please, Richard, keep it. Let at least part of me be close to your heart.'

He rolled his eyes at her girlish sentimentality but relented because he had been harsh, and he could see the shine of unshed tears she was bravely holding in check. 'I won't call you.'

'Yes, you will.' She sounded more confident than she felt. Surely after six months in a war zone he'd need a bit of female company?

'No, Pollyanna.' He picked up her hand and kissed her knuckles gently. 'I won't.'

CHAPTER ONE

Two years later…

Holly hadn't expected this morning to be quite so gruelling. But then anything, even sitting and listening to a series of boring lectures was hard going in the stifling humidity of Tanrami. She felt her enthusiasm begin to wane.

She listened to the army officer drone on and let her eyes wander to the view outside their green tented shelter. The sides had been rolled up to allow as much air to circulate as possible, but still everyone seated around her were fanning themselves with the pages of written material they had been handed this morning.

She looked at the leaden sky hanging over Abeil, the capital, and wondered if it did actually rain, whether it would help or not. Hot she was used to, Australia was hot, but this? At the moment, unacclimatised, it felt like she'd moved to hell.

She couldn't believe she was finally here. Her thoughts drifted to Richard, as they still too often did, and she couldn't help but wonder what he'd have thought of her ending up in a sweltering, typhoon-ravaged country. He had so often accused her of frivolity…well, look at me now, Richard. Look at me now.

After his parting barb she had determinedly knuckled down to her nursing career, still smarting from his damning summation of her life. But it just hadn't been fulfilling. Deep down

she hadn't felt like she had been making a difference in anyone's life. Modern medicine was all so rush and hurry. So the
opportunity to come here and really make a difference had appealed to her immensely.

Who could not be touched by the news reports night after
night? The images of so many people killed or displaced, their
homes and infrastructures totally destroyed, were heart-
wrenching. Super-typhoon Rex had cut a path of destruction
through the hundreds of islands in the group but Tanrami had
borne the brunt. Their plight had called to her. She'd felt…com-
pelled. There was no other way to describe it.

These were people who needed help and she wanted to be
part of it. Maybe Tanrami was a place where she could finally
get back to the basics of health care. Fundamentals like looking at the patient as a whole instead of a body part to be fixed.
Embracing individual cultures and beliefs and understanding
that sickness and illness were multi-factorial. And that you
couldn't afford to treat a patient in isolation to these factors.

The sky rumbled, interrupting her thoughts, and Holly wondered how much more moisture those black clouds could support. She yawned and sank lower in her chair, shutting her eyes
as she fanned herself. At least being seated right at the back she
could snooze unobtrusively.

Another khaki-kitted boffin was introduced and started talking to them about more safety issues. Enough already, Holly
wanted to stand up and bellow in an I'm-hot-and-bothered
voice. It's dangerous. We get it. There's a civil war going on and
there are rebels and landmines and diseases and mosquitoes.
But we came anyway. We want to help. Just let us get to it.

They'd been briefed and briefed and briefed! It had been
mandatory to attend lectures by the recruiting agency and the
aid agency and the Foreign Affairs department before being allowed to depart, and now it had been made clear that in order
to begin working they also had to attend the army briefing.

Most of the meetings dealt with the security situation in the country. She'd heard a thousand times about what dangerous criminals the rebels were. She'd heard it so much she almost felt sorry for them. In fact, she'd been following the political situation in Tanrami closely since deciding to volunteer. It seemed to her that the rebels were freedom fighters wanting to liberate their country from colonial roots.

Holly's excitement at finally making it here was being tempered by the heat and the repetitive, boring lectures. She just wanted to get on with it. The process had been too long as it was, a flood of volunteers overwhelming Aid agencies. Everyone had wanted to do their bit. Even with her nursing background it had taken three long months to place her at the orphanage.

The speaker finished and there was a smattering of polite applause. Next up was a mosquito talk and Holly, her eyes still shut, swallowed the urge to scream. How long would that take?

Richard was thinking the same thing as he took the podium. How many of these things had he attended since his deployment here three months ago? He looked at his notes and wondered why he'd bothered bringing them. He could certainly give his spiel verbatim.

Not that he disagreed with briefings. In fact, a lot of civilian aid workers were totally green when they arrived and they needed to be briefed extensively. It was just that he had so much work on back at the lab.

Now that the initial lifesaving stuff that they'd done in the first days and weeks of the disaster had been dealt with, a backlog of non-urgent tests had to be cleared. Not to mention the research he had been carrying out to monitor mosquito populations and test the effectiveness of the eradication plan he had spearheaded on his arrival in Tanrami.

Looking out at the sea of faces he could tell he wasn't going to hold their attention for long. They looked hot. And bored. Two major stumbling blocks to retention of information. He decided to ignore his notes and instead talk to them about his project. At least it was interesting and still managed to educate them about the dangers of malaria.

The speaker opened his mouth and uttered some words of introduction. Holly's eyes flew open. She'd know that voice anywhere. She'd dreamt about it and its owner so often in the last two years its timbre was instantly recognisable. It was Richard!

Suddenly the heat didn't matter, or the hours of boring talks—nothing mattered. Her eyes sought his face and drank the sight of him in greedily. She sat a little straighter. He'd changed. Even sitting right at the back she could see the differences.

He seemed harder somehow. Leaner. The grey streaking his hair more noticeable. The planes and angles of his face more pronounced. The way he held himself, more erect. Dressed in his uniform, dark sunglasses hiding his eyes, he looked completely without emotion. Like a machine. A military robot.

Sure, he'd always looked tough and forebidding but it was more than that now. His camouflage fitted him superbly, the red cross stitched to his shoulder denoting his status as a medic. His body seemed even more honed than previously. The uniform had always been a huge turn-on but today it seemed to create distance rather than invite her to touch. With his eyes shaded by reflective lenses, he epitomised the military image. From the way he carried himself to the authority in his deep voice, it screamed soldier.

He looked so…alone. So untouchable. What had happened in two years to make him appear even more unreachable than before? Holly felt her traitorous heart pick up its tempo.

Oh, no. No way! She was well and truly over Richard. She wasn't going down that track again. Particularly not with the new Richard. The old one had been hard enough to love. Her days of beating her head against a brick wall were over.

Still, the urge to call out to him, to have him look at her and fix her with one of those 'hey, babe' smiles was almost overwhelming. She shimmied down in her chair. She would not do that. She was here to help, not rekindle a relationship with someone who'd always been a bit of an unwilling partner in the first place.

And something told her he'd be none too impressed with her presence. It was best to just sit quietly and unobtrusively and sneak away at the end. After all Tanrami was a big place. There was no reason to think that they'd even cross paths. She should be able to finish her three-month stint without him even knowing she was here.

He talked on, oblivious to her turmoil. About his research and collecting specimens and the data he'd amassed about the mosquito populations in Tanrami. Also about malaria and its symptoms and treatment and the importance of taking prophylactic medication. The silky timbre of his voice slid over her skin and she was reminded of the times when he had laughed and teased. Looking at him today, she wondered if those times had actually happened or if she'd merely dreamt them.

Someone in front of her raised their hand and Holly tuned back into the content. She realised for the first time since sitting down with her fellow volunteers over two hours ago that they actually seemed interested in what the speaker was saying. Richard had engaged them which had been a big ask after hours of information delivered in a way that made it as interesting as watching paint dry.

'Yes, potentially specimen collecting is dangerous but probably more so out in the villages than in Abeil,' said Richard in answer to the question Holly hadn't paid any attention to. 'Most of my earlier work involved the villages further away and required more stringent security measures, but in and around

Abeil I generally go out by myself. Enemy forces are more likely to be a problem in the less-populated areas.'

Enemy forces? OK, enough already. Holly sat up a bit more. She'd sat through a whole morning of lectures about the protracted civil war and the bias was appalling. She felt her hackles rise further. Not Richard, too! Richard who, despite being a soldier, had always had a moderate, almost philosophical view of the world. It looked like more than just his physical appearance had changed. What had happened to him?

'Enemy forces? That's a bit extreme, isn't it?'

Everyone turned and looked at her and she realised that she must have spoken aloud. Oh, crap! So much for being unobtrusive!

'I'm sorry,' said Richard, pausing in mid-sentence and removing his shades. 'What do you mean?' He searched the back rows to locate the identity of the voice. It had been a while but its familiarity was ringing bells. Surely not?

As people in front and beside her parted he pierced her with a direct look from his black eyes and all her thoughts and feelings on the subject fled. Wow! She'd forgotten how impressive his eyes were! If nothing else, at least she had forced him to remove those damn sunglasses. She saw his eyes narrow as a flash of recognition streaked through them and then a very subtle flinch as his jaw clenched.

Oh, hell! Holly. Pollyanna was sitting in an army tent in Tanrami being briefed by him. What the hell was she doing in the middle of a disaster zone? Holly of the 'between things' fame. He remembered how harsh and dismissive he had been of her the last time he had seen her and couldn't believe she'd turned up here.

Silly girl! Didn't she realise these situations involved a lot of hard work and were potentially dangerous? That they weren't places you could come and play for a while as you flitted through life? That you saw things which could be traumatic and damaging?

'I mean that just because they hold different views from the general establishment, it doesn't make them the enemy.' She realised everyone was waiting for an answer and she managed to find her voice, swallowing to moisten her suddenly dry mouth.

Her voice was the same as he remembered. High with a sweet girly lilt. It was fresh and full of promise and…flirty. He remembered her saying she'd sleep with him because he was the sexiest man she had ever met and felt the familiar pull in his groin.

He suppressed the urge and focused on what she'd said, not how she'd said it. She was more Pollyanna-like than he'd given her credit for. Was she really that naïve? People who chose armed rebellion and took advantage of the chaos wreaked upon them by one of the world's worst natural disasters to further their cause were dangerous.

'Maybe not. But it does make them dangerous and not to be underestimated,' he said bluntly, placing his sunglasses back on his face.

He had retreated again. The machine was back and Holly was more than aware of the meaning behind his actions. Me soldier. You civilian. Me right. You wrong. How often had he taken that tone with her? Could she goad him back out of his glasses? 'Or maybe it just makes them misunderstood?'

Richard assessed her from behind his lenses. He didn't have the time or the inclination to go into the decades-old history of the civil war that had ravaged and held Tanrami back for too many years. A war older than Holly herself. All he knew for sure was the rebels were shaping up to be more of a menace than any of the international forces now stationed in Tanrami had bargained for.

Between hostage taking, stealing aid parcels meant for the poorest villages and hampering attempts to reach the most sick and injured, the forces had their collective hands full. Worse still was the nuisance of their landmines planted decades before and displaced by the massive storm surges that had swamped the area when Rex had hit during a king tide.

And Holly had just put herself amongst it. He felt the familiar urge to protect her rush through him and wondered how he was ever going to rest easy with her being so close.

'There are more effective ways to further your cause than armed conflict.'

'I agree,' she said, trying to stare him down despite the glasses. 'But when the other ways don't work, I guess they're left with little choice.'

He had underestimated her naïvety. His view of her as young and impulsive was confirmed. In true Pollyanna style she had added two and two together and come up with five. Even now at twenty-five she was seriously misguided.

'There is always a choice.'

She felt her stare being returned even though she couldn't see it, and quashed her dismay. Had he become some kind of military hard-liner? Or, worse, a mindless drone who accepted whatever his superiors fed him?

No. She refused to believe Richard didn't have a mind of his own. He had always been strong and sure and decisive. He'd never dithered or sought permission from anyone. Blind loyalty just wasn't him.

'Anyway...I think we've got ourselves off track,' said Richard.

He continued for a while longer and Holly was relieved to lose the attention of everyone else in the tent. She shook herself mentally. He was entitled to his opinion but it rankled and his obvious dismissal of hers found her in the midst of familiar emotions. How many times had she battled the fifteen-year age gap? Battled Richard's ingrained opinion that she was a mere child?

Holly stood at the end of Richard's talk, grateful that the briefing was over and they could finally go to their allocated jobs. Seeing Richard had been a complication she hadn't bargained on and the inequity that had existed in their relationship seemed even more glaring with two years' distance.

Refreshments were served in the tent and army personnel mingled with the new recruits. Richard made his excuses and slipped out. He had work to do and didn't have time to play benign soldier today. And seeing Holly again had disturbed him more than he wanted to admit.

From the moment she had burst into his life she'd always been difficult to ignore. How was he going to concentrate on his job knowing she was so near? Knowing she'd signed up for a dangerous role? He had to leave now before he sought her out and insisted she go home. She was a big girl and it was none of his business.

He rounded a corner and ploughed straight into her.

They apologised simultaneously as they disentangled themselves.

'Richard.'

Her voice floated towards him and he felt the same grab in his groin as before. 'Holly.'

There was silence for a few moments while they looked at each other. Their history faded from her mind as she took him in. Up close the changes were more evident. His hair had greyed considerably. There were frown lines on his forehead and around his mouth and a shuttered look to his eyes. It took someone who knew him intimately to see past the barriers. To see the damaged soul.

How was it was at all possible that with all these negative changes he was sexier than ever? His nearness reminding her of why she'd been so attracted to him. The solid broadness of his chest told her he was all man. Her previous boyfriends had paled in comparison. They had been mere boys.

'What are you doing here, Holly? It's dangerous.' Maybe he could make her see sense.

'I can handle it,' she said quietly.

'I thought you were between things? You should be out enjoying life. That's what young people are supposed to do. Not risking your pretty neck in a disaster zone.'

'A lot's happened in two years, Richard. I came to help. I need to help.'

'Don't be silly, Holly. Tanrami has plenty of helpers. Go be young while you can. Travel, buy nice clothes, sleep with lots of men—'

'I already own nice clothes,' she interrupted, dismayed that he was still treating her as a child. 'And if this isn't travelling then I don't know what is. As for sleeping with men, well, I think I've definitely come to the right place.' She couldn't help but goad him. 'Can't go wrong with five hundred soldiers just up the road.'

Richard scowled at her, appalled by the idea.

'Holly, you could see things here that are really very unpleasant. You're too young, too…happy. Go home before it damages you.' He couldn't bear the thought of her becoming jaded and cynical. Like him.

'I'm a nurse, Richard. I think I've already seen my share of unpleasant. And, besides, I think the Tanramans could probably do with a bit of happy.'

'I'm serious, Holly. This isn't a place you come to find yourself.'

Holly tried not to flinch as his blunt words fell between them. 'I've come to help, not to find myself. I've come to make a difference.'

She brushed past him, the moisture dewing her eyes a good match for the humidity. She had to get away from him. Her joy at seeing him again was suddenly crashing down all around her.

'Holly,' he called after her, immediately sorry for his harshness. She turned to face him and he was proud of the brave front he could see she was putting on. 'I'm sorry…it's just that you're too…'

'Young. Yeah, so you said.' And with as much dignity as she could muster, she turned on her heel and left him standing by himself.

Holly bustled through the back streets, cursing the heat and humidity. She felt the sweat trickle between her breasts and run down her abdomen. It was hot, it was humid and the air was rancid with months of waterlogged, decaying rubbish. All it needed now was to rain and her day would be complete, she thought. A warm, fat drop of water fell from the sky onto her face. Right on cue.

Walking around the devastated capital, she could see there was still so much to be done. Abeil, sitting right on the coast, had been a sitting duck for the fury of nature. Half of the city had been swamped and flattened by the massive storm surges that had thrown a good deal of the ocean at the city's primitive infrastructures.

Much had been accomplished in the time since. Rebuilding had begun but there was so much that remained to do. Large areas of debris in outlying areas had still not been cleared and bodies were still being found. Many had perished. Many more had died since as a result of disease, starvation and homelessness. And many children had been orphaned.

Which was why Holly was walking the streets of Abeil. She'd only been here for a fortnight but knew the routine backwards. Every morning two of the orphanage workers would walk into what remained of the old city of Abeil, follow an established route and pick up any orphaned children at designated checkpoints.

The locals knew the system and would be waiting for them along the way. Initially there had been many but the numbers had slowed to a trickle. A few times Holly had completed the two-hour journey empty-handed but on one occasion she had felt like the Pied Piper, a scraggly bunch of urchins trailing behind her.

Holly had separated from Glenda, one of the other aid workers, as they always did, to help shorten the route. She would meet up with her again at the ruins of the old Catholic church where they would continue for another half an hour before walking back to the orphanage.

But for now, as a tropical downpour appeared from the sky as if someone up there had flipped a switch, Holly sought shelter in an alley where the rickety construction of houses on both sides caused them to lean towards each other, reducing the torrent of rain from the heavens. She found a doorway to shrink even further into and managed to stay reasonably dry.

It wasn't such a bad position actually, she thought as she listened to the rain beat down on the tin roofs all around her. The noise was deafening, like a million drummers striking their instruments simultaneously. A breeze blew down the alley and her nostrils filled with the earthy smell of rain hitting dirt.

It was amazing how much the precipitation relieved the heated atmosphere and Holly revelled in the cool air on her face. It felt so good she was almost tempted to strip off her clothes and stand in the rain in her bra and knickers. Almost.

She pulled her baseball cap off, held it out, allowing it to half fill with water and plonking it back on her head. The water drenched her short fine hair, cascaded down her face, neck and shoulders and soaked into the fabric of her long-sleeved T-shirt. She looked down at the wet patch spreading from her neckline to her waist and sighed blissfully as the water cooled the sweaty skin beneath.

As quickly as it had begun, the rain ended, and Holly waited until she could no longer hear any pattering before she stepped out of the doorway. A noise further down the alley caught her attention and curious, she went to investigate. Maybe it was a child—lost and frightened and alone.

Like so many of the residential streets that made up Abeil, one alley led to another which led to another. The back streets were a maze of dingy alleys and dirt tracks formed around a mish-mash of lean-tos, huts and baked mud shelters.

She could hear voices now, muffled and speaking in the native tongue. She rounded a corner and stopped abruptly. The noises weren't coming from hungry children searching for food. They were coming from a gang of four boys who looked no older than fifteen. They appeared to be kicking at something on the ground.

It was a person! The inert form lay still as the youths continued their assault, oblivious to her presence. Holly felt temporarily paralysed as her mind tried to compute what her eyes were seeing. Her heart beat was loud in her ears. She felt sick listening to the dull thud of boots striking flesh. And scared and angry. They had to stop.

She strode forward on shaking legs, summoning the courage to help. She couldn't just stand there and let them kick a defenceless human being. She moved into the fray and felt her heart slam in her chest and hoped she could pull it off. Hoped they couldn't tell she was scared out of her mind.

'Stop that,' she said, advancing toward the scuffle. 'Stop it right now,' she demanded.

The youths stopped and turned to face her. A tall one with greasy hair and bad acne took a couple of paces towards her. He appeared to be the ringleader. After a few seconds he started to laugh. His mates joined him, a little hesitantly.

Holly felt chilled by their callousness. She didn't know the circumstances of what had gone on here in the alley and she didn't care, there were no excuses for such cruelty. Holly could now see it was a man on the ground and he still hadn't moved. Was he dead? The nurse in her demanded that she help him but the female was more than a little frightened of these brash, callous young men.

The leader advanced further towards her with a smile on his face that was far from reassuring. Holly swallowed nervously and held her ground. Great! Now what? She glanced over at the man on the ground again and was relieved to hear him moan and then cough. The youth said something in his own language and the rest of the gang sniggered.

Just then Holly heard whistling coming from where she had entered the alley and almost sagged in relief. 'Help,' she yelled in a loud voice, keeping her eyes on the leader who hesitated slightly. 'I need some help.'

Richard hitched his pack closer and kicked on some speed, sensing the desperation in the plea for help he had just heard. He rounded the corner at top speed and saw a tall youth startle as he burst on the scene. Richard's snap assessment of the situation stirred his ire. A gang of youths were menacing a woman. She was lucky he'd been in the vicinity.

'What the hell is going on here?' growled Richard, striding past Holly. The leader was tall but Richard was taller and meaner and trained in unarmed combat—he'd teach these boys to threaten a women.

The youths didn't hang around for their lesson. They disappeared quickly and Richard chased them for a short distance but stopped, knowing that his first priority was the safety of the civilian female he had rescued. The gang members had looked sufficiently petrified to think twice about doing that again.

Holly knew it was Richard the instant he'd spoken. Her relief at being rescued from a situation that hadn't been going well was tempered by the irony of who her rescuer was. Yet another sticky situation he had saved her from! Oh, well, beggars couldn't be choosers, and at the moment there were more pressing matters.

Holly rushed to the injured man's side. He was lying on his back and blood trickled from his nose and a wound near his temple. She felt for his carotid pulse and was alarmed by his stertorous breathing and the bluish tinge of his lips.

'Hey, mister, wake up,' she said, opening his eyes and noting his pupillary constriction to the bright light now filtering into the alley.

The man moaned in pain and coughed again, spluttering bright frothy blood on her shirt. That wasn't good, Holly thought as she hiked the man's shirt up and inspected the damage to his ribs. Definitely not good. The bruising was already coming out and Holly noted in alarm the flail segment of broken ribs on his left side.

She looked up when Richard ran back towards her and was so relieved he was by her side she almost forgave him their last meeting.

'Richard! Thank God. We have to get this man out of here and back to your hospital now.'

'Holly?'

Holly? He had rescued Holly? She wore baggy fatigues that hid her body and her cap covered her hair but it was definitely pixie-faced Holly. He felt his heart give a couple of loud thuds at what could have happened to her if he hadn't come along and wanted to yell at her and then shake her for good measure. This was exactly what he had feared.

The man on the ground coughed yet again and Richard felt his feelings ebb as concern for the stranger took over. Where the hell had he come from?

'What happened?' he demanded, kneeling on the other side of the patient, opposite Holly. His eyes met hers and he realised she had purple eyes. Purple eyes? Holly always did like to accessorise.

'Those boys were kicking him half to death when I found them. I think his ribs bore the brunt. He's got a flail segment.'

Flail? He dragged his gaze from her face and opened his pack, having noted the depressed section of ribs that was moving in and out completely asynchronous to the rest of the chest wall. It was severely impeding the man's ability to breathe.

Richard threw Holly some gloves and as he was putting his on, she reached for his stethoscope.

'Absent air entry on the left,' she said, pulling the stethoscope out of her ears with gloved hands.

Alarmed by the man's increasing dyspnoea and rapidly developing cyanosis, Richard assessed the man's neck veins. They were bulging.

'He's developing a tension pneumo,' Holly said. Richard didn't have time to be impressed by Holly's clinical skills as right before his eyes the stranger's lips lost their colour and his trachea slowly deviated to the right, shifting from its midline position.

'Get me a fourteen-gauge needle,' barked Richard as he tore the man's shirt right up the middle. 'He's got mediastinal shift, he'll be in real trouble soon if we don't decompress his chest, stat.'

She quickly located the large-bore needle and passed it to Richard, knowing that their patient's damaged lungs were leaking air into his chest cavity. His respiratory system was enormously compromised and his cardiac function would be next.

Richard methodically palpated the second intercostal space, running his finger to the mid-clavicular point, and plunged the needle through the man's skin and into the pleural cavity. There was no time for sterility, for preparing the skin with an antiseptic wash or even a local anaesthetic. The patient needed the air drained from his chest cavity so his lung could reinflate—now!

The effectiveness of the treatment was instantaneous. As quickly as it had deviated, the trachea moved back to its normal position. The patient's lips lost their cyanotic tinge and pinked up. He dragged in some deep ragged breaths.

Holly let out her pent-up breath. They'd done it. Their patient's condition had drastically improved. She started to feel shaky as reaction to the events sank in and the adrenaline surge ebbed.

She watched as Richard did a head-to-toe examination of the man, his capable hands running over the patient's body, thoroughly checking for any other areas of concern. She felt absurdly like crawling over, sitting in his lap and burrowing her head into his chest.

What would have happened if he hadn't come along when he did?

CHAPTER TWO

TWENTY minutes later an army ambulance carried the injured man back to the field hospital. Richard had radioed HQ and they'd stabilised him, padding his flail segment and inserting two IVs. Holly was acutely aware of Richard's arm brushing lightly against hers as they watched the vehicle until it disappeared from sight.

Without speaking, he marched back into the alley where all the excitement had occurred. Now it was all over he knew that if he opened his mouth she would feel the sharpness of his tongue.

Holly trailed after him. He was packing up his equipment and she knelt down beside him and silently helped. She passed him the stethoscope and as their hands brushed she tried to quell the familiar rush of sensation because they were in a dingy alley, in a foreign land, and it just didn't seem appropriate.

Richard's hand stilled as the contact reminded him of how tactile their relationship had been. He looked at her closely despite every cell in his brain telling him not to.

'You have purple eyes,' he said, because it was the first thing that popped into his head.

Holly had forgotten about the contacts she had put in that morning. The kids at the orphanage had loved them! 'Oh, yes...' she said. 'Just because I'm in a disaster zone doesn't mean I still can't look good, right?'

And she did. She really did. He stared at her for a few moments, a familiar heat building and invading every part of his body. He shook his head to clear the fog, remembering where he was and why he was there. He pushed himself up from the ground. He had to put some distance between them.

'We'd better get moving,' said Richard.

He picked up his pack and set off at a brisk pace. Holly practically had to run to keep up with his long-legged stride.

'So what were you doing out here?' asked Holly, trying to make conversation when it became obvious he wasn't going to talk to her.

'Collecting specimens,' he said.

'Mosquito water?' she asked.

He nodded briefly. 'Pleased to see you were listening the other day.'

She opened her mouth to compliment him on his lecture but almost as if he sensed her intention to talk he kicked on some more speed. While she was running to catch up she admired him from behind. His salt-and-pepper head bobbed with each footfall, his army camouflage pants pulling taut across his buttocks and his khaki T-shirt stretching across his wide back. His six-four frame was achingly familiar.

'I always listen,' she said, finally catching him up.

'Not that well, obviously. If you had, you'd know it's dangerous…a woman wandering around by herself.' He relived the awful moment when he'd realised that it was she he had rescued and the things that could have happened to her. It made him sick thinking about it. Just because they weren't in a relationship any more, it didn't mean he didn't care for her.

'I wasn't alone, we're not allowed. Glenda came with me, we just separated temporarily to shorten the trip.'

'So you were alone.'

'Well, technically…yes.'

'No technically about it. You were alone and that is not only dangerous, it's downright stupid. Do you have any idea what could have happened to you today?'

'I had to stop them beating him, Richard.'

'What?' Was she telling him she'd approached them?

Holly filled him in on what had happened. He shook his head. Just as he'd feared, she was going to get herself killed.

'Are you crazy?' he demanded. He opened his mouth to deliver another lecture on safety and her complete unsuitability for Tanrami but stopped abruptly when she squeezed his arm.

'Richard. Don't say it. I know that today could have ended very badly and I promise not to take any more risks. Please, just spare me the lecture. I'm OK. Nothing happened.'

'But it could have.'

'But it didn't. Got my own tough-guy soldier looking out for me,' Holly said, smiling at him.

Richard looked at her in exasperation. 'Holly, what happens next time…when I'm not around?'

'Cheer up Richard, it'll probably never happen.' This time she shot him a wicked grin because the conversation was getting kind of old. She'd been sufficiently scared to take heed.

Holly checked her watch. 'Shit, I'm late. Glenda will be worried.'

Richard smiled despite himself at her expletive. 'You work in an orphanage now, Holly. Language like that will see you go straight to hell.'

She cast her eyes around at the waterlogged city, the leaden sky, and drew in a deep breath of foetid air. 'Too late, Richard, I'm already here.'

She sighed and enjoyed the difference even a slight smile made to his face. It dimpled his cheeks and softened the planes and angles and the deep black of his eyes. It even made the dark stubble on his chin less military. It reminded her of the Richard she had first known and loved.

They found a very worried Glenda pacing outside the meeting point a few minutes later. Holly introduced them and Richard escorted them back to the orphanage. He listened to their idle chatter and made a mental note to talk to the CO about sparing someone each day to accompany the workers into the city on their orphan runs. He'd sleep easier if he knew a soldier was accompanying them. Not that he slept well at the best of times.

Richard plodded along behind them, trying not to ogle Holly's cute backside or the seductive sway of her hips. Even in baggy clothes she had a great strut. His mind wandered to how good she looked naked and then he shook his head, disgusted at himself.

Honestly, having her here was just the living end! He was here as part of an Australian Defence Force humanitarian mission. To monitor and eradicate mosquito populations. To treat cases of malaria and dengue and provide public health services and education. Not to pick up where he'd left off with a girl nearly half his age.

They reached their destination and Holly watched Glenda walk into the sturdily constructed stone building that had miraculously survived the typhoon and had been commandeered in the early days for use as an orphanage. All around them were the temporary buildings of various aid agencies, part of the massive international humanitarian response which had poured in after the devastating news had circulated the globe.

She could see the khaki tents in the distance that was Richard's field hospital and, further beyond that, myriad multicoloured tents stretched as far as the eye could see, a city full of displaced people, refugees in their own country, awaiting the agonisingly slow rebuilding process.

She looked at Richard who was looking anywhere but at her. He seemed to be finding the bustle of activity all around them particularly riveting. She also allowed the hubbub to distract her from her thoughts and the sudden awkwardness between them.

'Look, I'm sorry about before. While I think you took an unacceptable risk, what you did, confronting those boys was very brave,' said Richard.

He was a great believer in giving praise where it was due, and he had to admit her actions had surprised him. He knew from experience that a bug usually sent her into the vapours, and yet she had taken on a gang of violent teenagers.

Holly blinked, startled by the reluctant compliment, and felt stupidly happy. It had obviously cost him a lot if his serious face was anything to go by. She had the sudden urge to see him smile again. 'And me being so young and everything,' she sighed dramatically.

He gave her a grudging smile. Aha! That was more like it. 'I'd better go,' she said. 'I guess I'll be seeing you around.'

He watched her hips sway as she walked away from him. Watched until she disappeared inside the orphanage. Not if I can help it, Pollyanna. Not if I can help it.

Three days passed. Three days that lulled Richard into a false sense of security. He didn't see her, he didn't talk to her. He was beginning to think having Holly less than a kilometre away wasn't going to be a problem. Wrong.

'Sergeant,' said Gary Lynch, an army doctor, entering the lab area of the army hospital.

'Yes, sir,' said Richard, lifting his eyes from the microscope.

'I have customers waiting for you outside. Five children from the orphanage need malarial screening. I've just done physicals—they're all undernourished but remarkably well otherwise.'

And that's when his sense of security came to an abrupt halt. He just knew that Holly was out there also.

'Roach!' he called, returning his eyes to the microscope where he was examining mosquito larvae.

No one answered and he looked around the empty lab with

a sinking feeling. He was going to have to do it himself. He made a mental note to have Private Roach flogged and reluctantly left his desk.

He stood at the flap that separated the lab area from the outpatient section and looked through the clear plastic panel. There she was, with a bunch of rag-tag kids sitting patiently on the chairs provided.

Holly nursed an infant on her lap, one hand resting on its back. She was absently rubbing her face back and forth through the babe's soft downy hair. The child's hand rested on Holly's T-shirt-clad breast and had its head snuggled in her cleavage. It was a touching scene and Richard felt a pang somewhere in the region of his heart.

She looked up as he pushed the flap aside and smiled at him her purple eyes twinkling.

'Hello, Richard.'

'Holly.'

He stared at her for a bit longer. Everything about her was delicate, from her slender ankles to her heart-shaped face. Her blonde pixie-cut hair, feathering around her face, completed the picture. It emphasised her age, and Richard suddenly felt very old.

The child on her lap stirred, lifting its head up and swapping cheeks, pressing the other side to Holly's bosom. Richard couldn't keep his eyes off it as the child's hand settled back to rest gently on Holly's breast.

He looked back at Holly and realised she'd been watching him all along. Their eyes locked momentarily and it was suddenly as if they were the only two people in the world.

Private Roach brushed passed him and almost tripped as he did a double-take when he saw Holly. He stopped abruptly.

'You were looking for me, sir.'

Roach smiled at Holly and she smiled back at him and

Richard saw the gleam in the young private's eyes. He made a further note to use a cat-o'-nine-tails when Roach was flogged.

'I've left some slides under the microscope. Can you continue the classification process for me?'

Roach dragged his gaze away from Holly with difficulty, about to protest, but thought better of it when he saw the look of steel in his superior's eyes.

'Yes, sir,' he said, leaving reluctantly and shooting Holly another dazzler for good measure.

'Through here,' he said, and indicated for Holly to follow him.

She smiled at the children and stood and they followed her in their silent serious way. Holly had never met more solemn children. They had been through so much and her heart broke to think of how deep their sorrow must be.

'Up here,' said Richard, and patted an examination bench. The children stared at him with their big brown eyes. Apart from the baby, the youngest looked about three and the oldest around six. None of them moved.

Holly smiled. She was used to this blank, silent routine. It wasn't recalcitrance, just a mixture of a huge language barrier and powerlessness.

'Come on, my darlings,' she said, and smiled and nodded at them reassuringly. 'It's OK. *Jup, jup,*' she clucked, thankful that she was learning enough of the native language to get by.

Still they didn't move and her heart went out to them even more.

'What do we do now?' Richard asked, a smile playing on his lips.

He was wearing the same uniform as the other day and Holly tried not to be distracted by the broadness of his chest or the covering of dark hairs on his perfectly muscled arms.

'I'll sit up with them,' she said, and he helped her climb up onto the bench. She was still holding the infant, who was clinging to her.

The children watched the new development silently.

'*Jup, jup,*' she said again, and patted the space beside her. She turned back to him. 'Richard, you'll need to help them up.'

'OK, then, chickadees,' he crooned, crouching down to their level. 'Whose gonna be first? Who wants to sit next to Holly?'

Holly almost fell off the bench at the change in Richard as he spoke to the wary children. So he did have a soft side.

'I know,' he said. 'Who likes balloons?' He stood and drew a trolley closer that held various things, boxes of gloves amongst them. He pulled a few out, grinned wickedly at the kids and blew in the open end of a glove which he had narrowed into a neck with his finger and thumb.

The glove blew up just like a balloon except it had a bizarre udder shape to it as the five fingers inflated to their full length. Richard tied a knot in it and then turned it the other way round. Now it looked like a head with spiky hair and Richard completed the look by drawing a face on it.

One of the little girls giggled nervously and soon they were all laughing. He gave one to each child, lifting them onto the bench behind them as he did so. Suddenly they were chattering to each other and to Holly in their native language.

'Thank you,' she whispered, and hugged the now squirming baby to her breast. He wanted in on the act too and Richard handed him a glove balloon with a crazy face and earned himself a toothless baby grin.

While the noise of happy children filled the air, Richard told Holly what he was going to do.

'It's just a finger-prick,' he explained, 'I drop it onto the test strip and it reads in seconds. Like a urinary preg test. Think they'll be OK?'

'Not sure,' she admitted. The five kids had only come to the orphanage over the last couple of days and they still had trust issues.

'You're a nurse. You could help me. They might trust you more.'

'Oh, no. No way. Sorry, but I need to earn these kids' trust and I won't do that by sticking a needle into their fingers. Sorry, but you get to be the bad guy today.'

Richard could see her point but took up her suggestion that he run a test on her so they could see it wasn't going to hurt them. She held out her finger dutifully and he smiled to himself as the laughter died and five pairs of eyes focused on what he was doing to Holly.

Holly held her breath and tried not to flinch, both at the unexplained eroticism of Richard's gloved hand rubbing her finger and as the lancet pierced the tip. He squeezed out a drop of blood onto the test strip and then gave Holly a cotton-wool ball to blot the blood. He showed the kids the strip and they watched as the pink test line appeared.

'You're safe,' he teased in a low voice as the second line, indicating a positive result, didn't appear. He picked up her finger again, removed the cotton-wool ball, wiped off the smear of dried blood and covered the puncture site with a sticky plaster.

And then, because he couldn't help himself and he had an audience, he kissed her finger. 'All better now,' he murmured.

The children giggled and clapped, but Holly hardly registered them at all. Her finger felt hot, burning hot, as hot as the colour darkening her cheeks, and she sat pole-axed, momentarily stunned by his action.

'OK, who's first?' he asked the little ones.

The eldest girl held out her hand and he repeated the test on her. She didn't make a murmur when her finger was pricked and Richard knew that the others would be fine. These kids had been through so much more pain and suffering than a simple finger-prick. They were tough. Survivors.

'All done,' he said to the first girl, but she shook her head and thrust her finger back at him. 'It was good.' He nodded and smiled. 'All clear.' He nodded again, curling her fingers into her palm and placing them in her lap.

She shook her head again and thrust it back.

'I think she wants you to kiss it,' Holly suggested, coming out of the sexual haze his tiny kiss on her finger had caused.

Richard looked at her doubtfully and she shrugged at him. The little girl held her finger out solemnly. He sighed and pressed a kiss to it, sure that this went against every protocol he could think of. Still, the same went for kissing Holly but that hadn't stopped him.

The girl beamed at him, a huge smile of such utter happiness that Richard immediately forgot about the rules. The other children clapped again and Richard laughed and clapped with them.

He finished the other children in no time. The baby was more difficult and cried a bit when the needle pierced his skin but was easily placated by Holly. All the kids were clear and Richard was helping them down when an army nurse stuck her head through the flap.

'Sergeant, helicopter ETA fifteen minutes. Troops hit a landmine in their Jeep. Four critical. Sergeant Lynch wants you to stock up on fresh blood.' And then she was gone.

'I'll get out of your hair,' said Holly, rounding up her charges.

Richard waved the kids goodbye and then forced himself to turn away and not watch the sway of her hips and the wiggle of her cute bottom. He had a job to do.

CHAPTER THREE

HOLLY was outside, playing hopscotch with a group of children, when Richard passed by.

'Hey, where are you going?' she called out to him, and watched as he slowed then stopped and turned around.

He sighed heavily.

'Ignoring me isn't going to make me go away, Richard.'

'I wasn't ignoring you,' he lied.

'Oh, so you just…didn't see me.'

'That's right,' he said, swallowing another lie.

Holly wasn't fooled for a minute but she let it pass. 'Where are you going?' she repeated, walking further down the fence line so she was nearer him because he obviously wasn't going to come closer to her.

'Collecting some more specimens.'

'Pack looks kind of heavy.'

'I'm used to it.' He shrugged.

'Can I come with you?' she asked hopefully.

'No.'

'I can help you collect your specimens.'

'I don't need any help.'

'Have you ever, Richard?'

'I've been self-sufficient all my life, Holly. I don't need any-body.'

Apparently so!

'Which area are you going to?'

'The eastern side. You're not coming.'

'Cool. We haven't been to that sector for a while. I'll just let Kathleen know.' She turned away to head inside.

'I'm not waiting for you.'

'That's fine, I'll catch you up.' She shot him a dazzling smile as she disappeared out of sight.

Right. Like he was going to let her go wandering into the eastern side of the city all by herself.

'Oh, you waited,' she said innocently, reappearing a few minutes later.

Like she didn't know he would be waiting for her. He was pleased to see she'd got out of her scuffs and had put on some boots and thick socks. With her three-quarter length cargo pants and modest black T-shirt she looked kind of military and Richard tried not to go there. Women in uniform and all that.

'Shouldn't you have another worker with you?' he asked.

'Nah. Got a big tough-guy soldier by my side.' She grinned as she pushed open the gate and joined him.

Her purple eyes twinkled at him. He turned away abruptly, setting off at a killer pace.

'Are we trying to set a world record?' she asked, her short legs unable to keep pace with his.

'You wanted to come,' he said in a clipped voice, staring straight ahead, 'so keep up. Don't complain and definitely do not sprain an ankle or anything else typically female.' He couldn't bear emotional, scatty women who used their wiles instead of their heads. Way before Holly had come on the scene he had nearly married one and still felt blessed by his lucky escape.

She daren't ask what came under the typically female banner. She had a feeling he was talking about his mysterious fiancée that he'd alluded to on a couple of occasions when they'd been together but had steadfastly refused to talk about.

Whatever—he was letting her come so she scurried along, determined not to ask him to slow down. So what if she practically had to jog to keep up? She was fit, she would manage. 'So, talk to me about mozzies,' she said.

Richard relented and slowed his pace a little at the breathy hitch in her voice. 'What do you want to know?'

'Well, today, for instance, what's the purpose of collecting the specimens?'

'We're entering a critical stage at the moment. Any real problems with malaria and other mosquito-borne illnesses are going to explode if we don't monitor the situation and stick to our strategic plan.'

'Why now?'

'Well, it's been three months since the typhoon, right?' He looked at her and she nodded. 'Now what happened back then was that there were these huge storm surges, where the wind was so strong it whipped up massive waves and hurled them at the shore. And because Rex chose the worst possible time to hit, during a king-tide, the result was much more catastrophic. As these surges inundated the land they cleaned out all the mosquito breeding areas, just sucked them right back into the ocean, and all the fresh-water habitats that mozzies need to breed in were washed away and replaced by salt water.'

He stopped to see if she was following and she nodded at him again. 'It takes about three months for the salt to evaporate from these puddles and ponds and waterways and make them mosquito-friendly again. Plus with the monsoon season just getting into full swing, all the fresh water from the sky helps to quicken the process by flushing out salinity and leaving plenty of puddles and pools and even man-made receptacles for mosquitos to breed in.'

'What do you mean, man-made?'

'Oh, anything that will hold water. Things like buckets, bowls, discarded tyres, even empty coconut shells that the locals leave lying around fill with water in the rain. A lot of my job is public health education. Going into the areas where the locals are living and talk to them about not creating opportunities for mozzies.'

They reached an area that, even for Abeil, was exceedingly dingy. It had been the poorer section of the city but had survived remarkably well. It certainly wasn't anything to do with the construction of the dwellings because the whole area reminded Holly of a shanty town. It was pure economics. The more affluent you were, the more you were able to afford a home closer to the sea. So the eastern side through sheer distance alone had survived reasonably well.

'This'll do,' said Richard, pulling a map out of his pack and consulting it.

'Why here?' she asked, looking around and then trying to make sense of his map. 'What are all those shaded areas?'

'They're areas I've already collected specimens from.'

'So what do the specimens tell you?' she asked as she accepted the handful of yellow-lidded pots he gave her.

'It basically tells me if our earlier eradication programme has been successful. As I said earlier this is the most critical time to assess that. We look for, one…' he held out a finger '…if there are any larvae in the water specimens and, two, if any, what sort of mosquitoes they are. That way I can map mosquito populations and keep an eye on their progression and change or alter our strategic plan accordingly.'

'When did you become such an expert?'

She lifted an old discarded tin to find a pool of trapped rain water. She'd been watching Richard poke around in the rubble and rubbish and figured he'd tell her if she was doing something wrong. She opened the lid of a pot and scooped some of the water in. She handed it to Richard and he wrote on the label.

He shrugged. 'I've been working in malarial research for

about a decade now and had lots of field experience in Timor and Bougainville.'

Holly stopped mid-scoop. He'd been to Timor and Bougainville? Why had he never told her these things when they had been together? He had never talked about his job other than to impress on her his total dedication to it.

'You sound married to the job,' she said, stopping to observe his concentration as he made some notes in a notebook.

'I am,' he said, looking up and fixing her with a knowing stare, the lid of his pen still between his lips.

'Sounds lonely,' she said quietly.

'Nothing wrong with that, Pollyanna.'

She was about to object, tell him he was missing out on all the good things in life, when he turned away and continued his foraging. She sighed and shook her head. She'd had the conversation with him a million times already.

Holly returned to the job at hand in silence for a little while. But the quiet soon got the better of her and she had just opened her mouth to ask another question when a noise from behind stopped her. She was turning around when a low voice told her to stop. The request was backed up by the cold metal of a gun being pushed into her neck and a hand jerking her by the arm into an upward position.

'Tell your friend to throw his gun on ground,' the low voice spoke again.

'He hasn't got a—Yow!' she yelped as her captor twisted her arm behind her back.

It didn't even raise an eyebrow from Richard, who had wandered a little distance away and was staring intently into a dark hole.

'Ah, Richard,' she said, her heartbeat thundering in her ears so she was actually unable to hear herself say the words.

'Hmm?' he said, not turning around, not looking up from what he was doing.

'Richard!' she said louder, more insistent as the gun was pressed harder against her neck.

He looked up and, if the situation hadn't so serious, the look on his face would have been comical. Now she had his attention!

'What the—?'

'Stay where you are. Throw your gun on the ground. One false move and I'll kill her,' the man stated.

'OK, mate. Take it easy,' said Richard in a steady voice.

'Gun. Now!'

Holly jumped as the demand ricocheted around her ear canal. Her denial that he didn't have a gun died on her lips as he pulled something that looked like a pistol out from behind his back and tossed it a short distance away.

'Kick it to me.'

Richard did as he was told. The man said something in his native language and Holly watched as three men came from somewhere behind her and were suddenly all over Richard, patting him down then forcing him to kneel on the ground.

'Stop!' she said frantically, suddenly very frightened that they were going to execute him right in front of her. Her heart pounded in her chest. 'What are you doing? He's an Australian soldier, a medic, he's here to help the people of Abeil. Stop it! Let him go.'

The man holding her captive marched her over beside Richard and forced her to kneel, too.

Faced with her own mortality, Holly suddenly felt very angry. And scared. She was about to launch into an angry diatribe when she felt Richard's hand seek hers and squeeze. Was it for reassurance or a warning?

'What do you want from us?' Richard demanded.

Holly was amazed his voice sounded so calm. So in control. And for whatever reason he had held her hand, it had given her a measure of calmness as well.

When he got no answer Richard ploughed on regardless. He

felt fear but his priority to remove Holly from danger overruled everything. He had been in some hairy situations in the past, but he had skills and training and knew when it came down to it he could defend himself. But Holly? She hadn't signed up for this.

'Whatever it is, you don't need both of us. She's an aid worker. A volunteer. Let her go. You have me, you don't need her.'

Holly felt a lump lodge in her throat and decided right then and there, kneeling in the dirt of a foreign land, a gun pressed to her head, that if she died there today, she couldn't think of anyone she'd rather be with. Just his mere presence gave her courage in the face of such dire odds.

It was ironic on so many levels. That the man who had hurt her the most was the one she was going to draw her last breath with, and that somehow it seemed kind of…fitting. And it shouldn't. After all, the man in question still continued to dismiss her as being young and frivolous and it looked like she was never going to get a chance to prove to him otherwise. It just didn't make any sense to feel like this.

But holding his hand as she stared death in the face, she realised lots of things didn't make sense in this world. Not typhoon Rex, not kneeling in an alley, awaiting her death, and certainly not their convoluted relationship.

'Shut up and listen!' said the man who appeared to be the ringleader. 'We are soldiers from the Abeil Freedom Movement and you are prisoners of war.'

And then everything went black.

CHAPTER FOUR

THE dark sacks that had been placed over their heads were impossible to see out of and air flow wasn't great. It was stuffy and suffocating but Holly knew she could live with that. She was still alive and that was the most important thing.

Their hands were bound behind their backs and Holly could feel the pulses throbbing through her hands as the tightness of the rope constricted the flow of blood. They were yanked off the ground and forced to walk a short distance, stumbling and tripping because of their blinded state.

They entered some kind of dwelling where they were forced to sit on the ground next to each other while a heated conversation took place around them. Soon after they were manhandled to their feet again, the person 'helping' Holly letting his hand linger on her hip. She suppressed a shudder and refused to think about all the things they could do to her. There was no point dwelling on the what-ifs.

They were led outside again and then someone picked Holly up and placed her none too gently on her back against a hard metal surface and ordered her to lie still. She felt Richard beside her and quelled her rising panic. If he was with her, she could get through anything.

She remembered his earlier comments about typical females and guessed he didn't need to cope with histrionics from her.

It was a golden opportunity to prove to him she wasn't the young superfluous girly that he had pegged her as. If she could show him that she could be brave and level-headed and mature, then maybe, if they actually got through this ordeal alive, he would realise she was a woman. Not a child.

She heard an engine start and realised they were in a vehicle. They were being transported somewhere. Was that good or bad? She took a deep breath and tried not to think about what lay ahead.

She felt her ankles being tied together and for a brief moment she witnessed the grey, leaden sky as the sack was removed from her head. She took the opportunity to drag in some deep breaths of fresh air and orientate herself. They were lying in the back tray of a utility truck. Where were they going? A black tarp was secured quickly into place above them and once again they were effectively blinded.

'You OK?' Richard asked as they felt the vehicle start to move.

Holly could just make him out as her eyes adjusted to the gloom. A thin sliver of light shone into the space from where the tarp hadn't been fully secured at the tailgate end. It was tied back slightly and allowed fresh air to circulate.

Holly nodded because she didn't quite trust her voice.

'See if you can get out of your ropes,' he said as he worked away at his. 'Let's try and get out of here before we get too far out of Abeil.'

Holly nodded again because she was pleased that he was thinking about ways to get them out of the situation. She battled with her bonds for a while but it was no use.

'Richard,' she said into the silence.

'Hmm?' he said, still concentrating.

'Are they going to kill us?'

Richard stopped the frustrating activity and heard the note in her voice that said she was scared but trying to be brave. He marshalled his thoughts. He needed to keep her positive and focused on their freedom. 'If they'd wanted to kill us, they would have already done it.'

Richard's reasoning sounded sensible. 'Why are they doing it, then?' Holly just couldn't work it out. She'd been a good person all her life. Why the hell was this happening to her?

'What's the matter? Holly,' he said as he worked at his ropes. 'Losing faith in the misunderstood? Still think the rebels aren't the enemy?'

She stopped trying to free herself and gritted her teeth. He wanted to goad her into a political debate now? 'I still think that they have reason to be angry. Don't you? Or do you just blindly swallow the government line?'

'No, I don't. As it happens, I have a lot of sympathy for their cause. But I have absolutely no tolerance for their tactics.'

Yeah, well, she didn't have a whole lot of tolerance for their tactics at the moment either. It still didn't stop her from recognising that they had been wronged and feeling for their struggle. 'Have you ever thought that maybe they're driven to these tactics and that maybe they're not endorsed by all of their followers? Do you think we should tar them all with the same brush?'

Richard sighed and cursed himself for derailing his attempt at focusing her. 'Look. I'm sorry. OK? Maybe you're right.'

Holly didn't hear much conviction in his voice. They were both silent for a few moments, reflecting on each other's words. 'I suspect they're probably going to hold us for ransom,' he said into the silence.

Holly felt momentarily cheered by the thought and their apparent value to these people. And then she remembered that her government didn't negotiate with terrorists and certainly didn't pay ransoms. How long would they be held for before the rebels got trigger-happy?

'And when our government refuses to talk with them?'

'Hopefully we'll be long gone.'

He grinned at her and despite their predicament and disagreement she felt encouraged by his confidence.

Richard gave up on his ties and looked at the tailgate that was just beyond his feet. He wriggled down until they were touching and then he kicked with all his might. The utility looked fairly old and rusty from the inside so maybe the catch would loosen.

He kicked at it repeatedly, striking it with both of his feet simultaneously. Nothing. It didn't budge. He tried again. And again.

'I don't think it's going to work,' she said when he stopped for a breather. The noise produced by his efforts had been deafening and Holly was glad of the respite.

Richard kicked it once again out of sheer frustration. There had to be a way out of this. Think, damn it! Think!

The ride started to get really bumpy and Holly knew as she was bounced around that she was going to be covered in a million bruises come tomorrow.

'Where do you think they're taking us?' she asked.

'Into the mountains is my guess. It's their stronghold.'

Confirming Richard's supposition, the utility started to tilt as if going up an incline and she heard a gear change.

Into the mountains? Holly remembered seeing them in the distance from the back of the orphanage. They'd always looked so majestic, jutting from the earth in all their emerald glory. But seeing them, admiring their beauty and actually being among them were different things. Holly shivered. They had always seemed so isolated and she felt fear slide down her spine.

Richard saw the worry etched on her pixie face and sensed her apprehension.

'It's going to be all right, Holly. I promise.'

She swallowed the rush of emotion that rose in her throat and nodded. His confidence gave her hope. She gave him a half-smile. She would be brave.

He shuffled over to where she lay because she was a lousy

actress and her body betrayed her doubt, and he desperately needed her to believe in him. To believe that he would keep her safe at all costs. He needed her to trust him and to do anything and everything he asked of her to get them out of this alive.

He could do nothing at the moment but lend her some comfort and if that's what it took to allay her fears and forge some trust then that's what he would do.

'Roll on your other side,' he said.

'Why?' she asked, eyeing him suspiciously.

'Because you're scared, and if I had the use of my arms I'd hug you but as I don't we can spoon instead. It's not ideal but it might help.'

'You want to spoon me?' she asked. Half of her was incredulous at his request the other half found it, given their dire circumstances, absurdly funny.

'Yes.' He smiled.

'What, no flowers, no champagne?' She smiled back.

'I'm a fast mover.' He shrugged.

Holly laughed but did as he'd requested. A cuddle to calm the nerves sounded like just the right medicine at the moment. And let's face it, she thought, they could do little else.

It was a tricky process, changing positions while lying down with your hands tied behind your back in a moving vehicle, but she accomplished it with reasonable dexterity.

Once she was over she shuffled back and finally their bodies came into contact. She shuffled around a bit more, fitting herself to the shape of his body before she settled and relaxed.

Of course, that put her hands in the wrong spot altogether. Oh, dear, here she was, abducted by rebels, and all she could think about was how close to his groin her hands were nestled.

'Don't even think about it.' His low voice held unmistakable humour and she gave a half-laugh. The rasp of his chin stubble grazed her neck slightly and she felt her nipples stiffen at the erotic sensation.

'Maybe I'm a fast mover, too,' she said.

He heard the corresponding humour in her voice and chuckled. 'What? No flowers? No champagne?' And they laughed together.

They fell into silence for a few minutes. Holly squirmed a bit more because the ropes were chafing her ankles and biting into her wrists and it was difficult to find a comfortable position.

'For God's sake, Holly, can you stay still?' Bad predicament or not, he was just a man. One who could remember how good they were together as if it were yesterday.

'Sorry.' She ceased her struggle and found a position she could live with.

Richard was conscious of how big he was around her. She fitted against him perfectly, emphasising her smallness. Her head fitted snugly under his chin and he had to suppress the urge to rub it against her soft hair. How many times had they lain together like this?

Holly couldn't believe in their desperate situation she could feel so calm, but the familiarity of their position took her back to happier times. Snuggled into him, her naked flesh hot against his as they'd waited for the next inevitable surge of desire to choreograph their frantic coupling.

Richard could feel her trembling lessen and felt pride swell inside him. She had to be scared out of her mind and to her credit she hadn't cried once. She was doing a great job but lying this close to her soft body her frightened state was obvious and he needed her to continue to be brave and strong.

He cast around for something to say. 'So, tell me about what you've been doing these last couple of years.'

Holly filled him in on her nursing career, her midwifery, her work at the hospital and her growing disillusion with medicine. He listened without interrupting and Holly realised how much she had missed their conversations. Maybe he hadn't always treated her as if she were two.

The ute banged over a hole in the road and Holly felt her hipbone smash against the metal floor. She winced as the truck lurched and the movement flung them to one side, Richard's weight pinning her against the side.

The road smoothed out again and Richard eased back slightly.

'You OK?' he asked.

'No. I'm sure I'll be black and blue tomorrow.'

They settled back against each other again.

'What about you, Richard? How was Africa?'

'Hot.'

Holly felt his body tense around her. 'Something happened to you there, didn't it?'

Richard spent a good part of his waking life trying not to think about Africa and most of his sleeping life right back there again. Her intuition surprised him. Did it show?

'Africa is in the past. I prefer to think about the future.' And the only future he was interested in at the moment was their immediate one.

'And what's in your future, Richard?'

'Getting through this ordeal.'

His abruptness brought their situation back into sharp focus again. But it also seemed to intensify her curiosity. They were both living on borrowed time, surely he could open up a little?

'I mean if we get out of this. Is there a special person on the scene? Any little Richards running around?'

She held her breath suddenly afraid he would say yes.

'I think you know me better than that. I don't need a family, remember?'

Unfortunately she remembered only too well. Holly heard the utter conviction in his voice. So some things hadn't changed. Did he truly believe he could go through life totally alone? Completely isolated? What a chilling thought. She snuggled her body closer to his instinctively seeking his warmth and hoping, somehow, to convince him he was wrong.

'Everyone needs family,' she said wistfully.

'The army is my family.'

She'd heard that come out of his mouth so often yet still it horrified her. This was what she'd been up against. A man who was the product of a broken home that he wouldn't talk about. He had been offered a safe haven, a refuge in the ranks of the military. A man who felt indebted to an organisation who had offered him the closest thing to a family he had ever known. A man consequently married to his job. 'Oh, very personal.'

'A family has never been on my list of priorities, Holly.'

'Your priorities suck,' she said quietly, appalled at his callous dismissal.

'My priority at the moment is getting you and preferably me out of here alive. I cannot, I will not think about anything else.'

The engine cut out abruptly and there was no time for any more idle chit-chat. Holly felt hot acid burning her throat as fear slammed into her again. 'I'm scared, Richard,' she said in a quiet voice.

'I know, Holly, but you've got to be strong. It's going to be tough but you can do it. Just watch me and follow my lead at all times. You have to be prepared to make a break for it at any time, OK?' he whispered frantically, before their captors came for them. 'I need you to trust me and do anything I ask. I don't care how strange it seems at the time, OK?'

She nodded and then they heard car doors open and voices getting closer and the tarp was pulled back, flooding the tray with bright light. Richard and Holly screwed their eyes shut. Their captors dragged them from the vehicle and they stumbled and swayed until their eyes became accustomed to the light.

Behind the car a dirt road led back down a relatively gentle gradient through the foothills and eventually back to Abeil. Ahead was a narrow track, disappearing upwards into apparent jungle.

'Where are we?' said Richard stalling.

'The hills, Sgt Hollingsworth,' said the leader.

'And you are?'

'You can call me…John,' he said, and laughed, obviously amusing himself.

Holly felt a chill slide down her spine at the coldness of his laugh. John, or whoever the hell he was, had creepy written all over him. His age was hard to gauge but Holly thought he looked about fifty.

He had small piggy eyes and greasy slicked-back hair. His thin lips seemed to have an almost permanent sneer and his teeth were yellowed. A thin, hand-rolled cigarette hung from the corner of his mouth and Holly noticed he had matching nicotine stains on his fingers. He looked…evil.

'Where are we going?' Richard demanded.

'Up,' he said.

Holly looked at the mountain before her. OK, it wasn't Everest but it was quite a climb.

'Why have we been abducted?' he demanded.

'An Australian army medic and an aid worker? Come, now, Sergeant, you'll fetch a pretty penny,' John taunted softly.

Richard curled his fingers into a fist behind his back. John would pay for his smugness. 'Our government won't pay and you will be tracked down and brought to justice.'

Holly stared agog at Richard's defiance as John chuckled loudly, joined by his brothers in arms. Way to go, Sarge! Goad them into shooting us now. Good plan.

John turned to one of his crew and issued an order. The younger man scurried quickly away, going to the car and bringing back a digital camera.

'Say cheese,' said John, and he pointed it at them, snapping a quick photo, the flash somewhat out of place in the primitive jungle setting.

John nodded to the same man and he took the camera back to the car, got in, started up the engine and took off like a bat out of hell. They watched the car disappear and then John barked another order and two men undid their ankle ropes.

Next they untied her hands and Holly rubbed at her chafed wrists as she felt the blood rush back to her fingers in a wave, gritting her teeth at the painful hot prickling sensation as feeling returned.

'Let's go,' said John, and Holly felt a gun prod her in the back.

'Untie my hands,' said Richard, refusing to move.

'Sorry Sergeant, I'd be a fool to do that. You will remain restrained and one false move from you and I will shoot your friend without thinking twice. Now move.'

Richard ignored the painful jab of the rifle in his ribs and dug in his heels.

'You're right, Sgt Hollingsworth. We don't need you both. I could just shoot her now,' said John, cocking Richard's pistol and pointing it at Holly's chest.

Richard saw Holly pale and close her eyes, preparing to die. He waited for her to wail or beg or scream abuse at him, but she stayed bravely silent. Slowly Richard began to move and John smiled triumphantly.

They walked in single file up the narrow mountain track. Two rebels led them, their rifles slung over their shoulders. The one at the front wore Richard's pack on his back. Holly came next, then Richard, then John, followed by two more armed rebels.

After an hour of solid walking up the steady incline Holly's legs were screaming for mercy. She was relatively fit but this mountain goat routine was testing her limits and the track stretched ever upwards. Were they going right to the top?

Her muscles protested another increase in the gradient. How were they going to be tomorrow? All providing she was alive then, of course. She couldn't believe how blasé she was becoming where her life was concerned. Although when John had pointed Richard's gun at her it had been a different story. Her heart still hadn't settled from the rush of adrenaline.

Mind you, the climb wasn't helping her heart rate. All they needed now was for it to rain. Looking at the sky and glancing at her watch, Holly figured it was just about time for the mid-afternoon monsoonal downpour.

Richard had been planning and plotting like a man on a mission, the view of Holly's back keeping him focused on his goal—to get the hell off this mountain. Alive! The further up they went the more out of his control the situation became. John was clearly very clever and Richard knew he'd have to stay alert to outsmart him.

Richard was certain an opportunity would present itself. He just had to be ready. He noted the many side tracks that ran off the main route down either side, like narrow tributaries snaking off a big river. Were they just formed from soil erosion during the monsoon or were they alternate pathways, short cuts even, that the rebel forces used when needed?

'So, John,' said Richard breaking the silence, 'you speak remarkably good English.' He may as well try to get as much information as possible.

Holly startled. Birds and insects had been the only sounds until now. She noted the distinct lack of puff in his voice. Maybe the man really was a machine?

'Thank you, Sergeant.'

'May I ask where you learnt it?'

'Australian schools are excellent Sergeant, but I guess you know that already.'

Richard was far from cheered by the leader's generosity in sharing information with him. He had expected to gain nothing useful—after all, John was too clever to give away important identifying facts. Unless…he already knew their fate. Richard's mouth set into a grim line. Not without a fight, Johnno. Not without a fight.

'I'm surprised an educated man would be party to such futile, thug tactics,' Richard goaded.

'Desperation can bring out the thug in us all, Sergeant. There has never been a better time to promote our cause. The whole world has witnessed Abeil's tragedy. We would be foolish to not take advantage of the free publicity.'

'Surely your cause is better promoted through political means. You must know you will only get the world off side through abducting us.'

'It is difficult to seek a political compromise when we are considered criminals and dismissed out of hand. Forty years of struggle and still a free state of Abeil remains elusive, Sergeant. We grow weary of the wait.'

'I still don't understand what you hope to gain from holding us hostage. As I've already said, our government doesn't negotiate with terrorists.'

'So, now we are terrorists. So much name calling.' Richard didn't have to turn around to see the smile on John's face. He could hear it.

'You are much more valuable to me than you know, Sgt Hollingsworth. It's not just the price we can put on your head.'

About to query the cryptic comment, Richard was cut off by a sudden deluge from the heavens. He was drenched in seconds. They all were. The noise of the rain was thunderous and drowned out all other sounds for the half-hour it lashed down around them.

Holly was just visible in front of him, struggling against the storm, slipping often on the track as dirt quickly turned to mud. She was doing so well. Much better than he'd expected a woman to be doing. She still hadn't cried or had a tantrum. She hadn't even broken her ankle.

If Holly had found it hard going before, it was almost impossible in the rain. The ground was slippery, making the route suddenly treacherous. Visibility was bad and she was frightened she'd stumble and plummet right off the edge down the sheer drop on either side. Her clothes weighed a ton and her boots and socks felt like they were made of lead. Her thighs and calves ached.

She wanted her mother. And a cup of tea. And a warm bed. She wanted to close her eyes and for this all to be a bad dream. So she did the only thing she could do in this sort of situation. She cried.

Oh, she was quiet about it. She didn't beat her chest and shake her fist at the heavens, which was exactly as she felt like doing. She felt the hot tears well in her eyes and let them run unchecked down her cheeks.

There was so much water running down her face no one would be any the wiser and there was too much noise to hear her muted sobs. She would be all right in a minute. She just needed to release all her fear and anxiety and frustration. Then she could be brave again. She had to stay in control for Richard, so she could do whatever had to be done, but just for the moment she wanted to indulge her oestrogen and be a girl.

As the rain tailed off so did the incline and Holly sighed with relief as the strain on her aching muscles eased. They were walking along an almost flat area now that undulated gently from time to time. The track was wider and she didn't feel like one wrong footfall, one slip, could mean instant death.

The two rebels in front of her held their weapons high above their heads as they entered a puddle that lay across the track. Holly thought it rather strange until she realised that the puddle was deeper than it seemed. They were hip deep in it before she could blink.

Holly sighed and trudged in, too. She refused to think about the bacteria and parasites and the myriad creepy-crawlies that were probably swimming around her in the soup-like brown water.

She could tell her almost pathological fear of creepy-crawlies was going to get a real workout in the jungle. Not quite the way she'd hoped to confront it! Richard, who had been privy to her bug paranoia on more than one occasion, had enough to worry about without her squealing every time an insect landed on her!

The water became waist deep and her boots sank into the thick mud at the bottom grabbing at her feet each time she lifted one, making her progress twice as difficult. Every time something brushed her legs she had to suppress a scream. Did they have piranhas in this part of the world? Or water snakes?

She waded out the other side and turned and looked behind her at Richard, who was having to complete the chore with his hands tied behind his back. She wanted to wade back in and help him, despite having only just thought she never wanted to repeat the experience. She started to do just that but was prevented from doing so by a gun pushing into her ribs.

He smiled at her, a smile that said, I'm OK, it'll be OK and keep your chin up. The smile she gave him was kind of weary before she was prodded onwards again. She wanted to scream at them to leave her alone and let her rest but she remembered Richard had told her to keep her mouth shut so she set it in a grim line and plodded on.

Richard kept his eye on Holly's soaked form in front of him. He knew it was taking every inch of her courage to walk through the dirty water and not dissolve into hysterics. Holly didn't do insects or any kind of creepy-crawly. Yep, she'd be totally freaked by now.

How many spiders, cockroaches and other household insects had he'd killed at her insistence? Poor creatures innocently going about their business, unaware of the size-twelve boot descending upon them.

Holly lost track of the number of puddles and creeks they walked through. Each one seemed worse than the last, and she doubted if she'd ever been more drenched or more freaked out in her entire life.

Just when she thought she could go on no further, a clearing appeared ahead and she smelt the woodsmoke before she saw the fine wisps trailing heavenwards. As they approached, people came out to greet the soldiers and look curiously at the prizes they had brought with them.

Not that she felt like much of a prize. She was exhausted. Every muscle protested. She was soaked and her hair bedraggled. She longed to sit down and the sight of the fire burning in the background called to her on a primal level.

Pigs, chickens and the odd goat roamed freely around the central area. Young children eyed them with inquisitive stares, giggling and pointing and then running away to play. The camp was alive with noise—animal sounds, children's laughter, the crackling of the communal fire and adult chatter.

Somewhere in the background a woman screamed. Holly wondered for a moment if she was delirious because nobody seemed to be paying it any heed. The noise stopped, to be replaced by muted wailing and moaning. The unknown woman was obviously in pain. What was happening to her? Was somebody torturing her? Was that why no one seemed to give a damn?

'Why is that woman screaming?' demanded Richard. He had heard her pain and distress too, and his thoughts were running in a similar vein to Holly's.

'Relax, Sergeant,' said John, his voice full of derision. 'She is in labour.'

Holly almost sagged in relief, and she saw Richard's shoulders visibly relax. That certainly explained it. Holly had heard enough labouring women to be confident John was telling them the truth. She also knew that different cultures handled labour pain in their own ways. Still, her distress rang around the clearing and Holly hoped everything was OK.

'We will rest here for the night,' said John. 'We'll set out in the morning for the next camp.'

'Higher?' said Holly because the mere thought made her want to join the labouring woman and howl like a banshee.

'Higher,' he confirmed, and nodded to one of his colleagues who prodded them with his rifle butt, herding them into a rickety wooden shelter with a dry earthen floor. Some sort of woven fronds formed the roof and a fire burned in the middle of the floor surrounded by a ring of stones.

A door shut them in and through the wooden slats they could see two armed guards posted at the door.

'Are you OK?' Richard asked her.

Now was not the time to dissolve into tears but the concern in his voice was almost her undoing.

'Sore and tired,' she said quietly, 'but, still, I think I'm better than her,' she said, indicating the renewed screaming they could hear.

'Untie me,' he said, turning and presenting his imprisoned wrists.

'Oh, God, Richard, I'm sorry,' she said, attacking the ropes quickly. It took her for ever to undo them. The rain and Richard's attempt to loosen them had tightened them to the point of impossible.

'Richard, what a mess. Do they hurt?' she gasped as she pulled the last knot free. She lightly stroked the bloody rope burns encircling his wrists, pulling her fingers away as he winced at her touch.

'Like you wouldn't believe,' he said, assessing the damage himself. If he'd had his kit he could have dressed them properly, but he was just going to have to try to keep them clean and pray that they didn't get infected in the moist jungle environment teeming with bacteria.

There was a bucket of water sitting next to a pile of wood in one corner. It looked fresh and the bucket clean so he dipped the edge of his shirt into the water and squeezed it out over his wounds.

'Here, let me,' Holly offered, and knelt beside him.

She scooped small palmfuls of water and sluiced them over his wrists. It felt cooling and soothing and stung like hell all at the same time. She was gentle and he looked at her bowed head and his heart did a funny flutter thing that had no place in the predicament they were in.

'So, what happens now?' she asked, looking at him suddenly and catching him looking at her. She felt a constriction in her chest at the puzzled look she saw on his face.

'If we can't escape tonight, I guess we go higher.'

'I can't, Richard.'

'Sure you can.' He smiled at her. 'It's amazing what you can do with a gun poked into your back.'

'Do you think the outside world knows about us yet?' she asked, sitting on the floor, satisfied his wrists were as clean as she was going to get them.

'They might not have received the picture yet, but Kathleen and my CO are going to know we're missing. And Kathleen knows we were together. I suspect they're probably already searching for us.'

'And they're going to look for us here? In the mountains?'

'Once a ransom demand is made and it becomes clear the rebels are holding us, I'd say this will be the first place they'll look. Unfortunately there are quite a lot of mountains in this region and they cover an extensive tract of land.'

'So…we're screwed? We're going to die. It's over.'

'Absolutely not. Come on, where's that Pollyanna attitude? It ain't over till the fat lady sings.'

Another scream broke the humid air and Holly got the giggles. It wasn't exactly singing and it was only temporary fat but it was ironic nonetheless. Still, as omens went, it seemed kind of ridiculous so Holly didn't see the point in worrying. And

when Richard's deep throaty laughter joined hers, the seriousness of the situation faded.

'Come on, then,' said Richard after their laughter had petered
out. 'Socks and shoes off. Let's try and get our stuff dry before
we have to get going in the morning.'

Holly followed suit, wringing the excess water out of her
thick socks and laying them in front of the fire next to her waterlogged boots.

'It'll be dark soon. Once the camp settles for the night you can
take your damp clothes off and dry them properly by the fire, but
if you sit near enough you should be able to start the process.'
Richard imparted this information very dispassionately. Whatever
else he did, he must not think of a near-naked Holly or let her
know the thought terrified him more than all the rebels in Abeil.

Richard was right. Darkness descended quite quickly and
delicious smells from the communal campfire they could see
through the slats of their prison made Holly's mouth water. Her
stomach grumbled loudly and she realised she hadn't had anything to eat since breakfast.

Her hunger almost took her mind off their situation and then
the woman having the baby would cry out again and it was all
brought back into sharp focus. They were in the middle of the
wilds, held hostage by a rebel army, and their future was un-
certain at best.

At least having Richard by her side stemmed the hysteria that
threatened every time she thought about their circumstances. Her
arm rubbed against his as they sat with their backs to the fire and
she yearned to snuggle into the circle of his arms and draw the
quiet strength and confidence he exuded so effortlessly.

The door opened a little and a woman entered with two bowls
full of plain rice. Holly devoured hers as if it was the grandest
offering fit for a king. There was nothing in the bowl that re-
sembled the aromas coming from outside but it was something
to fill the stomach and beggars couldn't be choosers.

'I think we should get some sleep,' said Richard after they'd finished eating. 'How dry are you now?' he asked.

'My shirt and bra are dry but my cargos are still a little on the damp side.'

'Why don't you take them off and lay them in front of the fire for a while?' He tried not to let her see his concern at the thought of seeing her bare legs. 'I'll turn my back,' he offered hastily, and promptly did just that.

Holly stared at his back. She hadn't picked him as a prude. For goodness' sake, all he'd see was a bit of leg and now he was making her feel self-conscious. She quickly slipped her cargos off and spread them on the ground. 'What about you? Surely your fatigues are damp too?'

'I'll survive,' he said, his back still to her.

'Richard, I have seen naked men before.'

'I really don't want to discuss your sex life, Holly.'

She shook her head at his back and snorted. 'I meant I'm a nurse, Richard. But, hey, if you're having problems getting sex and me off your mind—'

'I do not have sex with you or anyone on my mind,' he snapped, turning to refute the point and immediately wishing he hadn't. Her legs were every bit as spectacular as he remembered. Petite and shapely. Standing before him in a black T-shirt and black, barely there knickers, it was suddenly easy to forget that two armed rebel soldiers were less than a metre away.

'Good, because I'm too tired and all that screaming is giving me a headache. I'm going to sleep,' she said, lying on the earthen floor a little way from the fire and turning her back to him.

Her hipster briefs rode up one cute butt cheek and Richard stared at the creamy flesh, mesmerised. Well, he couldn't take his trousers off now. There were things inside that were being more of a soldier than he was at the moment!

He followed her lead and turned his back to the fire, positioning himself close to the door so it couldn't be opened without him knowing. He tried to find a spot on the rock-hard ground that was the least uncomfortable. It certainly brought more meaning to the saying between a rock and a hard place!

Holly was exhausted. A deep exhaustion that seeped into her bones. She couldn't remember ever feeling so weary. Not even the regular screams that continued to come from somewhere behind them could stop her eyes from closing. Although somewhere she registered that they were more loud miserable moans now and that the woman seemed to be tiring. Too exhausted to find the energy to scream.

Well…she could certainly relate to that!

CHAPTER FIVE

RICHARD awoke to the door being opened onto his ribs. He sprang to his feet and took an immediate defensive position.

'Easy, Richard,' warned John, pointing the pistol at him, ever-present cigarette hanging from his mouth. 'We need your expertise.'

'What expertise?' he asked, hearing Holly stir behind him. 'Get dressed,' he said to her curtly, and turned back to John while still blocking the doorway.

'The labour isn't going well.'

'I'm no midwife, John. Don't you have someone here who usually handles that?'

'We used to but she didn't return to the camp after the ty-phoon. We assumed she was one of its many victims. Even the rebels lost people to the sea, Sergeant.'

'I'm a midwife,' said Holly, coming to stand by Richard. She swayed as she fought off the cloud of exhaustion that still hung heavily over her head. Her eyes felt gritty and sore.

'No,' said Richard, barring her movement.

'Yes,' she said. She took some comfort from the fact that he was obviously protecting her, but whoever the labouring woman was she needed help. 'It's OK, Richard. I want to help.'

'Good,' said John. 'You come,' he said to Holly, 'You stay,' he said to Richard. 'Don't think of doing anything funny. My guards will kill you without hesitation.'

'One moment,' she said, and quickly removed her contacts. Her eyes felt like they were on fire and something told her she'd need to concentrate. She flicked them into the fire, feeling a momentary pang. They hadn't been cheap but…there was no need to accessorise in the middle of nowhere.

Holly was led to a shelter similar to theirs further up the track. Every step was agony as her rested muscles protested their reuse.

'This is Mila and her mother Kia,' introduced John.

Holly smiled at the women confidently, trying not to betray her inner turmoil. She'd completed her midi last year but had been so disillusioned by obstetric intervention that she hadn't practised as a registered midwife.

'What's the problem?' Holly addressed Mila, who was lying on a low bed and looked completely and utterly exhausted. She looked so young, barely a teenager, her large belly dwarfing her.

'Kia says the baby is stuck,' said John.

'How long has she been in labour?' Holly looked at her watch. They'd already been here for about eight hours.

'Three days,' said John after consulting with Kia.

Holly had to stop herself from gasping. No wonder the poor girl looked so weary. Her mind raced. A prolonged labour, a small mother and a large baby. If the baby was truly stuck, in such primitive surroundings there would be little she could do. She needed to check its position first.

'I need Richard,' she said to John, 'and his medical kit.'

'No. Just you.'

'She needs rehydrating and if this baby arrives as flat as I think it will, it'll need some resuscitation. I need Richard and his bag. Now.'

John nodded sullenly and left. Richard was back in one minute.

'You got fluid in that bag?' she asked, barely acknowledging his presence.

'Saline, Haemaccel, Hartman's.'

'Get a cannula in her. Give her a litre of Hartman's. Any gloves?'

Holly was relieved to put the latex protection on. She knew from the briefings there was a high level of STDs among the locals and HIV was also prevalent. She hadn't wanted to come into contact with the girl's bodily fluids until she had protected herself.

She inserted a finger and could feel the baby's head right there. She was almost at the end. But what kind of shape would the baby be in? Was it still alive? This far down the birth canal a heartbeat was difficult to detect even if she'd had the right equipment.

An oil lamp gave reasonable light and Holly was glad for Richard's expertise as he easily slipped an IV in and hooked up some fluids.

'Let's run it in fully open,' said Holly. 'Once she's had it I want to get her up off her back. Get her squatting and see if we can get the baby moving with a position change.'

The fluid took fifteen minutes to run through during which time Mila had ten contractions and the baby remained stubbornly unmoved. Richard bunged the peripheral cannula and, with the help of John translating, they encouraged a slightly rallied Mila into a squatting position. Holly encouraged Kia to sit on the low bed behind her daughter and allow Mila to lean back against her between contractions.

Once Mila had adopted the best pelvic opening position, the head delivered quite quickly, despite Holly's best efforts to slow it down. The last thing she needed was for Mila's perineum to tear. How would she stitch it?

Luckily it didn't happen. How, Holly would never be able to say because the head was huge! Even badly moulded and looking rather cone shaped it was amazingly big. If this baby wasn't over four kilos she'd eat her hat.

As she lay down on the floor to get a closer look, Holly wondered if Mila had gestational diabetes. It would explain the huge baby and, particularly with no ante-natal care, the diabetes would have been largely uncontrolled.

Holly felt her heart rate settle, knowing they were over the hardest part. Only she was wrong. So wrong. It became quickly apparent that the shoulders were now stuck fast. Holly groaned inwardly. Shoulder dystocia? To think she had been worried about a perineum tear! This was much more dire. Much more fraught with complications.

She shouldn't have been that surprised, given the circumference of the head. The shoulders were obviously too broad to descend through the pelvis and the anterior shoulder was probably caught on one of the pelvic bones.

As far as obstetric emergencies went, this was up there. The cheeks of the baby puffed as a contraction tore through Mila but the baby, which should have just slid out, was stuck fast. Holly knew that the cord was being compressed as each second ticked by compromising the baby's oxygen supply.

She found herself yearning for the obstetric services that were on tap at a hospital. The very thing that had frustrated her as a student midwife was the one thing she needed now more than anything else. An obstetrician.

'What's wrong?' asked Richard. He had seen the play of emotions on her face and knew something wasn't good.

'Shoulder dystocia.'

'Oh.' He may have had limited obstetric experience but he knew enough to know it was a potentially life-threatening condition.

Luckily Holly had firsthand experience with dystocia. She'd been the only midwife in her student group who had witnessed a dystocia delivery.

He brought the oil lamp down closer to the action. 'You can do it, Holly,' said Richard quietly, and squeezed her arm.

She looked at him and looked at the faith on his face and she just knew that she'd walk over hot coals to prove him right. So, she wanted an obstetrician. Well, she didn't have one. She had herself and she had Richard—and she could do this. They could do this.

'Richard, when this baby comes out it's going to be flat as a tack. I'm going to need you to do the resus while I keep taking care of Mila. OK?'

'OK,' he said.

She hadn't expected such a confident reply and his conviction crystallised her thoughts. She straightened her shoulders. If he wasn't fazed then neither was she—they could do this.

Holly inserted a finger to see if she could loosen the shoulder off the shelf the pelvic bone had formed. She prodded and pushed and tried to rotate with no success, and as the seconds ticked by she knew the baby was getting closer to asphxia. She tried to gently rock the baby's head, hoping to dislodge it from its position. A bit like easing a cork out of a wine bottle. Still no success. Still the clock ticked.

An episiotomy was what she needed. A surgical incision into the perineum used to create more room by widening the birth canal.

'What are you thinking?' Richard asked, watching the concentration puckering her brow.

'That I wished I had the facilities to do an episiotomy.'

'I have suture material,' he offered.

Holly hesitated for a second and looked around her at the primitive conditions. 'It's too risky. If she haemorrhages from the site she'll die, and then there's infection.' She cast another look around her with the eyes of a nurse and saw potential bacteria sources everywhere.

She felt overwhelmed suddenly and cast Richard a helpless

look. Richard understood how she felt. Working in less than ideal conditions was almost second nature for him, but Holly was used to having a gamut of medical equipment and personnel on hand. He understood how alone it felt to be the one every one was looking to.

'Got a plan B?' he prompted.

His calm voice intruded on her helplessness. She looked at him and drew strength from his assuredness. She nodded. She had one more manoeuvre up her sleeve. She had to try and deliver the posterior arm to make room for the opposite shoulder. And if that didn't work she was going to have to perform the episiotomy and pray it didn't all go to hell in a hand basket.

He squeezed her arm encouragingly. She drew strength from his faith and turned back to her task. She took a deep steadying breath and inserted as much of her hand into the vagina as she could. She located the arm she needed, flexing it at the elbow and sweeping it up and across the baby's chest until it was delivered.

She didn't have time to congratulate herself. No time to rejoice. She had to hope she'd created enough room to rotate the body and apply downward pressure so the shoulder could finally be delivered.

And it worked. The shoulder cleared and she pulled the baby free of the birth canal. She lifted it up, looking at the not-so-little boy, momentarily triumphant before his pale face and silent mouth registered and she passed him hastily to Richard.

Richard's hand shook as he accepted the wet newborn. Holly had done her bit now it was his turn. OK. This was not his usual area of expertise but the ABCs still applied.

'Rub him vigorously with a clean cloth. Clear his mouth with your finger. Pinch his nose and sweep downward to remove all the mucus.'

Holly prattled off the orders as she continued to lie on her side on the floor, tending to Mila. Her eyes hadn't left her patient. Kia handed Richard a cloth and he did as he was instructed. Still the infant remained unresponsive. He could feel a slow carotid pulse.

'What's the heart rate?' she asked, looking at him momentarily, her ears tuned for a cry and becoming more alarmed at not hearing it.

'Forty.'

Their eyes locked for a second, sharing the seriousness of the situation. 'Don't let this baby die now, Richard,' she said.

Richard moved into action. Its heart needed to beat faster and he knew he was going to have to initiate some external cardiac massage and give the babe some breaths.

He lay the baby on the cloth on the ground and, using the tips of his index and middle fingers, rapidly pushed the centre of the baby's chest. His injured wrists protested the movement but he ignored them. He puffed some breaths into the baby's lungs by placing his mouth over the baby's mouth and nose. Once, twice, three times.

And then the baby coughed and then he spluttered and finally took a breath. The joyous noise of lusty cries filled the air and everyone in the shelter, everyone in the camp, breathed a collective sigh of relief. He watched as the baby pinked up rapidly, waving its arms around, apparently furious at its traumatic entry into the world.

He handed the baby boy to Mila, whose sobbing had turned to joy. She took him eagerly despite her exhaustion. Both Mila and her mother were crying, gabbling away at each other and talking to Richard and Holly with huge, broad grins.

'They are thanking you,' said John, cigarette drooping from his bottom lip.

She was relieved to see the baby waving his right arm around like nothing had ever happened. A high percentage of babies born with shoulder dystocia ended up with impaired or no movement in their affected arm. All the tugging and twisting and pulling required to get the baby out could stretch and irreparably damage the brachial nerve plexus situated in the baby's neck.

Thankfully there had been good outcome achieved tonight. Better than Holly had dared to hope for. But what if the baby had died? She glanced up at a very dispassionate John, his cold eyes watching her through a thin trail of smoke. Would it have been a death sentence for them if the baby had been stillborn?

Back in their own shelter again, Holly looked at her trembling hands and felt the muscles in her legs turn to jelly. She was shaking all over as she sat down and thrust her hands towards the warmth of the fire. The air was quite cool now and reaction to the events had chilled her even more.

'That was amazing, Holly,' said Richard, feeling on a real high, momentarily forgetting their situation.

Holly saw the gleam lighting his black eyes and recognised it instantly. It was the buzz that only witnessing the birth of a baby could give you. She knew that look intimately and it reminded her of the reasons she had become a midwife in the first place. Before the politics and power games of obstetrics had jaded her.

She only wished she could return it. At the moment she was feeling too…strung out. It had been a huge day. Being taken hostage had been bad enough, but the stress of holding a baby's life in her hands had been much worse. With the adrenaline rush over, all the what-ifs surfaced. She felt absurdly like crying again and the fire blurred before her eyes.

'You were amazing,' he said, and smiled at her.

She blinked rapidly. 'I was scared out of my mind.'

She shivered as a cool breeze caressed her bare arms. The pale skin puckered and she rubbed the flesh to warm it.

Her admission caused him to look at her, and he saw her blank expression and the weariness in every line of her body as she sat hunched by the fire. His old protective instincts stirred. 'You're cold,' he stated.

'A little. I'll just move closer to the fire,' she said dismissively because she was too emotionally raw at the moment to take his kindness. Suddenly all she wanted was for him to take her in his arms and kiss her and that made her feel even more wretched, because she didn't understand why she'd feel like this when there were so many more important things to think about. Like her life.

He shrugged off his long-sleeved fatigue shirt and draped it over her shoulders.

'I'm all right, Richard,' she restated in a firm voice. 'It's no problem. I'm not cold.'

The shirt was heavenly. It contained his body heat and his smell and she wanted to bury her face in it. Distant memories were being triggered. How many times had he comforted her when she'd needed it? Held her when she'd been upset? Kissed her better when she'd been hurt? He may have always kept a frustrating emotional distance but he'd never denied her physical closeness.

Accepting his gift would move her into dangerous waters. She was just managing to keep it together and as much as she was over him their situation was extraordinary and she needed a little human comfort now more than anything. The urge to feel his lips on hers was growing so powerful she could almost taste him.

'I said no, Richard,' she snapped, and shrugged the shirt off her shoulders so it lay in the dirt behind her.

'Hey. What's wrong?' he asked, gently grasping her chin and forcing him to look at her.

'Besides being kidnapped by rebels and dying for a cup of tea and being scared witless that baby was going to die and wanting my mother, you mean?'

'Is there more?' he asked, trying to make a joke, but he could tell by looking into her eyes that she was tired and fragile.

'Yes, actually, there is. I'm sitting next to a man who has no idea that just taking his shirt off for me makes me want to kiss him so badly I want to scream. But he doesn't want to kiss me, in fact, he dismisses me outright as just some young little piece of fluff. None of which should matter to me because we're stuck in the jungle with armed rebel soldiers at every turn, and it's highly likely I'll die from a rebel bullet long before sexual frustration claims me, but…there you go…that's how I feel.'

Oh, boy! She wasn't kidding when she said there was more. His gut lurched as her admission about kissing him twisted inside him. If only she new how tempted he was!

'I'm sorry for dismissing you as a young little piece of fluff because what you did tonight was incredible. And for what it's worth, I do want to kiss you, Holly. Very much. But nothing will change the fact that I'm fifteen years older than you and you want things I can't give you.'

'And what would you do if I just leant over and kissed you?'

At the moment he'd probably kiss her right back because she looked so small and fragile and feminine by the firelight, and that appealed to him on levels he hadn't even known existed. And she'd lain in the dirt tonight and refused to give up when a defenceless life had hung in the balance, and that appealed even more.

Richard swallowed. 'It would be a mistake, Holly.' He hoped he sounded more convincing than he felt.

The fire seemed to crackle louder between them, the insects outside grew noisier as the silence inside the shelter stretched. To hell with him, she thought, and moved her head, her lips, a little closer to his.

'Holly,' he warned quietly, when he could feel her breath mingle with his. 'Don't do this.'

'All you have to do is move away, Richard,' she whispered, staring at his lips.

She was right. All he had to do was get up and move away. Now. Right now. But…he couldn't. And he needed her to see it was wrong.

'Holly, please. It's not the time or place.'

He saw her shut her eyes, and he drew in a deep ragged breath as she moved her body back from his.

'Holly—'

'Don't, Richard,' she said quietly, turning her back to him and settling herself on the ground. 'I'm tired and tomorrow I'm going to be forced at gunpoint to climb another mountain.'

He touched her shoulder lightly. 'Holly.'

She shrugged it away. 'Don't touch me.'

Richard spent the rest of the night dozing, waking frequently, throwing another log on the fire and checking that Holly was OK. He told himself he was too alert, too wary to give in to the black abyss of sleep, but in his gut he knew he was scared. Too scared to sleep lest he should dream the dreams that haunted most of his nights.

He didn't want Holly to see his vulnerability. She had to believe he was strong. Invincible. That he could get them out of there. She thought he was a tough guy and that worked to his advantage. If she saw him at his worst, the strung-out mess his nightmares always reduced him to, she might lose faith in his ability to get them out of this alive. And that was to be avoided at all costs.

Richard was awake at the dawning of their second day of captivity and watched as the camp stirred to life. The first rays of sun poked through the canopy heating the moisture-laden air. Even this early, the jungle hissed and steamed around them.

He glanced at Holly, the early morning light filtering through the slats casting shadows against her skin. She'd rolled on her back and her shirt had ridden up, revealing her flat midriff and delicate waist.

He stared because he couldn't help himself. Her small high breasts, outlined in all their perfection by the T-shirt, rose and fell in unison with her respirations. Her mouth had relaxed and looked soft and very kissable.

He felt a stirring in his groin that by itself wasn't so unusual at this hour of the morning but had nothing to do with his diurnal rhythms. It was the memory of last night's kiss or near kiss. He could feel the anticipation, the longing as strongly this morning as he had last night. And even hours later, knowing he had done the right thing, it didn't lessen the impact.

Holly stirred and stretched slightly, recoiling instantly and becoming fully awake.

Her eyes came to rest on Richard sitting propped against the wall looking like hell, and she knew she wasn't just waking from a really bad dream. She was living it. Fortunately the intense pain in her legs overrode any lingering embarrassment from his rejection last night.

'I can't move, Richard,' she groaned. She really started to panic then. No way could she manage more mountain climbing today. Would they shoot her if she couldn't…wouldn't? Or would they let her crawl on her hands and knees?

Richard heard the agony in her voice. He knew how badly her muscles must be hurting today. Luckily for him, part of his job involved strenuous physical tests and pushing himself to the limits of endurance.

Today's journey was going to be a particularly horrific form of hell for her. Worse than yesterday. She needed to rest but that wasn't going to happen, and if they had a good opportunity to escape she would have to run. Run hard. There was nothing for it, she needed to warm her muscles up first.

'Stay where you are,' he ordered as he crawled to where she lay. He picked up her legs and plonked them across his lap.

'What are you doing?' she asked, half sitting, trying to remove her legs from contact with his body.

'I'm going to massage your calves and thighs. It's the only way you'll make it today.'

'Forget it. I'm never going to make it,' she protested again, trying to remove her legs and wincing as a sharp pain tore through her leg muscles.

He started to knead her calf muscles, knowing that they were too sore for her to move them away again. 'You can make it,' he said as his long fingers worked at the bunched fibres.

'I can't,' she whimpered as his fingers created agony and ecstasy in equal measure. Tears of pain stung her eyes and she swiped them away.

'You can and you will, and when I see a side path or an opportunity I'm going to yell at you to break. You're going to react instantly and run like the wind and we'll be free.'

His pep talk was more for his own benefit than hers. If he could treat her like one of his men, he could ignore that the flesh beneath his fingers was smooth and supple instead of bulky and hairy. That her ankle was delicate and her knee slim and the fact that her thighs led to an entirely different place to that of one of his men's.

Despite the torture, Holly had to remind herself that rebel soldiers were a mere metre away. Because if she didn't and she could actually physically get up without collapsing in screaming agony, she'd jump his bones, whether he liked it or not. His ministrations were so erotically painful she didn't know whether to scream or to purr.

Kia entered just as Holly thought she was about to drool in the dirt. She smiled at them shyly as Richard released Holly. She had brought them some breakfast and it smelt so delicious Holly knew she'd drag her aching body over an acre of broken glass to get to it.

Through their limited knowledge of each other's language Holly managed to ascertain that the baby was doing well and that Mila was recovering nicely. Holly could tell Kia had sympathy for their plight and she wondered if that could be useful.

When Kia came back to retrieve their bowls, Richard indicated he wanted to speak to John. Now they had gained some kudos with the delivery of Mila's baby, Richard felt it was time to exploit their deed for all it was worth. If he could find out where they were going and what the rebels had planned for them, it would have been a worthwhile exercise.

'You rang?' said John, standing at the doorway several minutes later, a sardonic smile in place.

Richard walked outside and away from Holly. 'We saved a child's life last night. How about you reciprocate and let us go?'

John laughed and it disturbed some birds nesting in the jungle canopy. 'Sergeant, you amuse me. Good try.'

'OK. Release Holly. You'll still have me. Consider it a gesture of good faith. Our government will look favourably upon it.'

John laughed again. 'Do you really think you were a random selection, Sergeant? We've been watching you and your mosquito foraging forays into Abeil for weeks. The red cross on your shoulder makes you very useful to us. Yes, we can get money for you. We can buy food and medicine and weapons, but as I've already said you are far more valuable to us.'

'Oh?' said Richard, intrigued despite himself.

'Fumradi is ill. He needs medical attention. We chose you.'

'Fumradi? The rebel leader?'

'Very good, Sergeant.' He smiled cynically. 'You are well informed.'

'Take him to a hospital.'

'No hospitals. He would be arrested as soon as he was admitted.'

'Take him to the army hospital. We treat anyone, regardless. It's part of our mandate.'

'No hospitals.' He dropped his cigarette and ground it into the forest floor. The steel in his voice would have done a sergeant-major proud.

'OK,' said Richard, holding up his hands. 'So let me get this straight. You abduct me at gunpoint, threaten my life, restrain me and keep me under lock and key, and expect me to treat one of the people who perpetrated—worse, who no doubt ordered—this crime against me?'

'You are astute, Sergeant.'

'You could have just asked. This cross,' he said, pointing to his sleeve, 'means, regardless of who you are or what you've done, I'm honour bound to treat you. How far away is he?'

'We will get to top camp tomorrow,' said John.

'So, what's wrong with your leader?'

'He was wounded two days ago in battle. He is a very brave man.'

Richard knew there were still skirmishes that occurred daily in the disputed territories between government and rebel troops. He also knew that the rebels had used the chaos and confusion caused by the typhoon to reinvigorate the fight for independence.

'He has a fever now,' John finished.

Great, thought Richard. How the hell did they know that he was even still alive? Fever meant infection and infections could be deadly. 'Did someone remove the bullet?' he asked.

'I did,' John said.

'What if he's already dead when we get there? By the time we reach him another four days will have already passed. If his wound is infected it may be too late.'

'You'd better hope for your sake he's not, Sergeant. If you are of no use to us then we'll have to revert to plan B and see what your government is willing to pay.'

'They won't pay,' said Richard, his voice matter-of-fact.

'Then I guess you're in a spot of bother,' said John, and gave a sickening chuckle.

'Two conditions,' said Richard. 'I won't be bound. I won't be locked up. I give you my word I will not escape. I will treat your leader but not as a prisoner, as an Australian soldier doing the job he came here to do.'

John considered it for a moment. 'Granted.'

'Release the woman.'

'No way, Sergeant. The woman is my insurance policy. She stays. That is not negotiable. When Fumradi is better we will release you both. I give you my word.'

'No deal.'

John laughed again and Richard was actually chilled by the harshness of it. 'You think I won't shoot her now, Sergeant? You want to test me on that one? Better still, I could leave her here alone with some of my soldiers that have a particular liking for white women.'

Richard felt the bile rise in his throat.

'You'll treat Fumradi whether she's alive or dead, because that's the kind of person you are. It's up to you what happens to your woman.'

Richard walked right up to John, closing the distance in an instant and grabbing the front of his shirt. He dwarfed the older man and took pleasure in the fleeting glimpse of fear he saw in the man's eyes. He heard the cocking of guns and the demands in a foreign tongue that he had no trouble translating, as nearby soldiers became nervous.

'You touch one hair on her head, she gets a scratch and everything that this cross stands for…goes out the window.'

John grabbed Richard's hand and forcibly removed it from near his throat. He took a step back. 'So we understand each other, Sergeant. You do your bit and I'll do mine.'

Richard turned away, not trusting himself to answer. Their situation had drastically improved. They would be kept alive while they were useful but the threat to Holly's safety, her life, burnt in his gut.

'If you can't save our leader, all bets are off,' said John to Richard's retreating frame.

Richard slowed and turned, the dank, sizzling heat of the jungle reflecting his seething mood. 'Oh, I can save him, John. And I will hold you to your promise. You can bet on that.'

CHAPTER SIX

EVERY step Holly took was agony. Even on level ground her calves and thighs screamed at her, but this steady incline was excruciating. To make matters worse, the humidity was oppressive. Sweat ran down her face and arms and trickled between her breasts.

They were largely protected from direct sunlight by the sparse canopy overhead, but the heat and the moisture made the march hard going. Holly felt as if she was constantly pushing against a wall of wet blankets.

The knowledge that they had been taken for a purpose didn't fill her with as much joy now as it had when Richard had first told her about it that morning.

'See,' she had said, 'not such bad people after all.' And he had given her a scowl.

But it didn't take her too long to figure out that Richard was the valuable one. Her capture had been purely incidental—she had been in the wrong place at the wrong time. So she wasn't needed. Putting it bluntly, she was expendable.

As he marched, Richard forced himself to concentrate on what he had in his pack that would be useful in treating his patient instead of how much he wanted to deck John. And how much he wanted to shake Holly.

Fluids and clean dressings. And antibiotics. But only a very limited stock of these lifesaving drugs, enough for one dose of each. If Fumradi's wound had gone septic it wouldn't be enough. It could buy them some time but getting a raging infection after his initial injury, one dose of antibiotics was like throwing a hand grenade at the Great Wall of China, hoping to reduce it to rubble. It just wasn't going to work.

Well, there was nothing he could do about it now. He had given his word that he would treat Fumradi and that's what he would do. For the moment at least, if nothing else, it gave them a potential reprieve.

Suddenly they heard helicopters overhead and John halted the party, ordering them all to get down low and stay still. Richard looked up and through the trees could make out the familiar shape of a Blackhawk.

'Is that one of ours?' Holly asked turning in her crouch position to Richard.

'Yep.' He smiled.

Holly smiled back at him and felt hope for the first time since this whole ordeal had begun. Even her muscles stopped aching for a magical moment. 'They're looking for us?'

'Absolutely,' he confirmed, and hoped he was convincing because he wasn't really sure. It wasn't unusual for Blackhawks and Iroquois to fly over this region. 'They know we're missing and they're searching for us, Holly.'

And the relief in her eyes and the smile she shone his way was worth it. If it gave her the impetus to keep going, if it gave her one small ray of hope that they would get out of here alive, he knew he would tell her whatever she needed to hear.

They heard the *wocca, wocca* of the rotors grow distant and John ordered them up again. Holly was amazed at how much lighter her step was. How the knowledge that there were people beyond this mountain who knew of their plight and were trying to help could spur her on and reinvigorate muscles that had previously been begging her to stop.

Richard noticed the spring in her step instantly. He'd been forced to watch the sway and wiggle of her bottom all morning, a different kind of torture, and definitely recognised a renewed perkiness.

They trudged on silently for another hour. Richard noticed Holly's steps becoming slower again. Had the jubilation caused by the chopper receded already? She tripped over a tree root and he heard pain in her muttered expletive. He needed to try to keep her spirits up.

'Tell me about your work at the orphanage.'

His voice startled her out of her misery. The only voices she'd heard for a while had spoken a foreign tongue and it felt good to hear English. And she was grateful for anything that took her mind off the burning in her legs. So she prattled on about her volunteer job for a while.

'Is it rewarding?' he asked when she had run out of things to say.

'Working with the kids, sure. I feel like I'm making a real difference, which is a nice change.'

Richard could relate to what she was saying. That was the part he liked most about his job. The fact that he made a difference to the lives of so many poor people caught up in such awful situations.

'But I don't think anything could have prepared me for the overwhelming sense of despair and hopelessness of these poor people. The scale of the destruction… I suppose I sound like some spoilt rich girl,' she sighed, sploshing through her millionth puddle in the track.

He laughed. 'You are.'

She laughed back. 'I guess you're right. I don't live in a disaster zone, and I have a wonderful family who are all alive and well so, compared to these poor people, I guess I'm pretty rich.'

In his book, that made her a millionaire. The gap that had always existed between them yawned ever wider. Just one of the reasons their relationship had been doomed from the beginning. They couldn't have had two more contrasting backgrounds if they'd tried. No wonder she looked at the world through Pollyanna eyes.

They trudged on, a companionable silence falling between them. 'Your turn,' said Holly.

'Oh, no.' Richard laughed.

'Come on, Richard, I've just spoken non-stop for half an hour. Talk to me about something.'

'Like what?' he asked.

'Tell me about your childhood.'

Great. Let's start with something easy, he thought. 'I don't think so.'

'Oh, come on, Richard,' she said, trudging around a rocky section of the track. 'I already know it wasn't the Waltons. We were an item for two years, I did manage to figure out some things. I hardly know anything about you. Indulge me. Did your parents divorce?'

Richard couldn't help the snort that escaped him. She seriously thought that divorce was the worst thing that could happen? She wanted to know? OK.

'My father was a wife-beater, my mother was a drunk. I raised myself. My father died in a bar brawl when I was twelve, and my mother drank herself to death a couple years later.'

Holly faltered. She'd had no idea. She'd occasionally seen past his tough-guy image and caught glimpses of hurt but this was so much worse than she'd ever imagined. When he had told her through tight lips that he'd come from a broken home she'd just assumed divorce. 'Any brothers or sisters?'

'No, thank God. That's about the only thing my parents did right. I think the fewer children that were exposed to my home life, the better.'

'So, you really have no family?' she asked incredulously. She hadn't believed him when he'd said so previously. She'd just thought he was estranged from them. How awful. How lonely.

'I told you already. The army is my family.' He heard the pity in her voice and couldn't keep the curtness out of his. He didn't need her sympathy.

Well, of course, the army felt like his family when they'd probably been the only true support system he'd ever had. They'd given him stability, safety and a shot at a career. And discipline and direction. More than that, knowing the man he had become, they had obviously also given him pride and self-esteem.

All the things that a family were supposed to give you but didn't if you were a kid from a dysfunctional home. She was finally starting to understand him.

But the facts of the matter didn't make his statement any less tragic. 'Oh, Richard,' she said, turning to face him, 'that sounds terrible. So…sad. Why did you never tell me?'

'I didn't need your pity then, Pollyanna, and I don't need it now. So don't waste your tears on me. I like my life just fine.'

'But there must be someone else. Anyone. Not just your job.'

'Nope.'

'What about your ex-fiancée? Surely she was your family?' Holly held her breath. He'd refused to talk about her when they'd been together. Holly hadn't even known until an army mate had let the cat out of the bag. 'What was her name?'

Richard sighed and gave in. If talking about his personal stuff kept her going then so be it. 'Tanya,' he said. 'She was very young.'

OK, so that's where his age hang-up came from. Holly mulled that over for a bit. He'd obviously been stung badly once before. Why had he never told her this stuff? Why had he waited until they were marching up a mountain with trigger happy rebels? Damn his he-man façade.

Richard felt a resurfacing of all his old angst and was surprised it still affected him a decade later. Yes, Tanya had been young but he had handled it badly. He should have stuck with his gut feeling all along and realised that a guy with his background made lousy marriage material. Kept his distance. Like he had with Holly.

But Tanya had been so pretty and she had been crazy about him and he had desperately needed someone to love him and someone to love in return. He'd just chosen the wrong girl and it had been a painful lesson to learn.

Holly's heart went out to him as she trudged along the track. How important would it have been to him to have made that relationship work? After the emotional void of his early years? She could sense his feelings of failure like a tangible aura.

'So, what happened?'

Richard sighed and rubbed his hands through his hair. He really didn't want to get into it. But one look at her straighter back and quick, easy strides and he knew that he'd bare his soul completely if it distracted her from her pain.

'She hated me being away with the army, which I was, quite a bit. I got posted to Darwin, which horrified her. I went up there to get settled and she was going to follow a little later. But I came home unexpectedly one day to surprise her, and found her in bed with another man.'

Holly gasped. Stupid girl! 'Oh, Richard,' Holly said, turning to face him, walking backwards. 'What did she say?'

'That it was my fault. That she was young and had needs and I was never around to fulfil them and no way was she ever going to move anywhere. And that it was over.'

Holly felt awful for him. 'I don't understand why you never told me any of this stuff when we were together.'

'Why would I?'

Holly turned back to the track. She felt her sympathy evaporating. She was getting ticked now. Had she meant so little to him? 'Because that is what people in relationships do, Richard. They share stuff like that.'

'Not me. I only told you now to keep your mind off your muscles and keep you putting one foot in front of the other.'

Holly felt like screaming. He was still treating her like a child. But as she trudged on, silently fuming, she had to admit their chatter had kept her mind of her aching body. Half an hour later, with her muscles starting to protest again and the road ahead disappearing ever upward, she broke her miffed silence. She was going to have to talk to him or throw herself off the mountain. Neither alternative appealed.

'So, how come you're still a sergeant?'

Richard stiffened and forced himself to keep going. 'I like being a sergeant.'

'I thought one of the reasons you were so keen to go to Africa was for the promotion opportunities. Isn't it every soldier's ambition to become a…brigadier or something?'

He smiled, easing the tension that had sprung into his muscles at the mention of Africa. 'I'm happy with my rank.'

'You always struck me as being more ambitious than that.'

'Sorry. I'm not.'

'Really?'

'Really.'

'It's just that you seem to have so much experience and expertise.'

'Look,' he said, becoming exasperated by her persistence, 'trust me on this one. I could be in the army till I'm one hundred and I'll still only be a sergeant.'

'How can you be so sure about that?' she said, wiping the sweat of her forehead with an even sweatier arm.

'Because…' He hesitated, wondering if he wanted to go into it, 'there was an incident in Africa…'

Aha! So she'd been right. Something had definitely happened while he'd been away. Something that had made him harder. More unreachable. Holly waited for further explanation. None seemed forthcoming. 'What sort of an incident?'

'I…broke some rules,' he said, trying to keep it as vague as possible. He really didn't want to think about it. He avoided thinking about it at all costs. It was bad enough that his dreams took him there most nights. He didn't want to talk about it in the daylight hours. 'Suffice to say promotion isn't ever going to be on the cards for me.'

'But—'

'Holly,' he interrupted, 'I don't want to—'

'Talk about it,' she finished.

'Bingo.'

Holly huffed out a frustrated sigh. Bloody men! Did he really think he was doing himself any favours by keeping things to himself? She stomped up the incline now. His tough-guy act wasn't fooling her. She remembered her shock at seeing him again. At how he seemed so much more distant. Machine-like even. Whatever it was, it must have been big.

'Well, I think they're mad.' She stopped abruptly and turned around and he almost careened into her. 'Surely the army is crying out for good leaders? People who are intelligent and dedicated and good at their jobs? I don't care what rules you broke. If you deserve a promotion, then it should be yours.'

Richard was surprised at the depth of her feeling. They were standing really close and her voice had husked over as she'd spoken. He couldn't believe she was showing him more forgiveness and loyalty than the army had.

John growled at them to keep moving and they turned back to the gruelling task of climbing higher. They stopped for a quick snack when the sun was directly above them and then hiked for another three hours in heavy rain.

Holly was relieved to finally reach another campsite and they were again herded into a structure similar to the one at the last camp. Holly didn't care. She was grateful to have stopped moving and sat on the hard earthen floor like it was the comfiest sofa in the world.

She pulled her socks and shoes off as Richard stoked the fire and wrung out the water from her socks. She lay back on the ground, her knees bent, revelling in the luxury of a horizontal position. Not even everything she had learned today could keep her from shutting her eyes.

'Oh, Holly, your feet!' exclaimed Richard.

She roused from the comforting layers of sleep that had quickly claimed her and half sat up. She had large, red, ugly blisters on her heels and over the bony prominence on the side of each big toe.

'Don't they hurt?' he asked, lifting each foot and inspecting the damage.

'Not as much as you yanking my sore legs around.' She winced. 'I didn't even know I had them until just now. I think the pain everywhere else is too intense to notice.'

Richard watched her fall back against the ground and shut her eyes again. She looked totally exhausted. 'I'm going to get my pack and dress those blisters,' he said, and wasn't surprised when she didn't respond.

Richard pushed open the door and the two guards placed restraining hands on his chest.

'I want my pack. I want to talk to John.'

The man appeared before him miraculously. 'Yes, Sergeant?'

'I need my pack. Holly has some bad blisters, I'd like to dress them.'

John spoke to one of the soldiers beside Richard and he left. He returned quickly with the requested pack. Richard picked it up and started to take it with him back to Holly.

'Oh, no, you don't. You take out what you need. We'll keep the pack.'

Richard felt his ire rise and gave John a mutinous stare. 'I gave you my word we wouldn't escape.'

'Take only what you need. The pack stays with me.' John's steely voice brooked no argument and Richard bunched his hands into fists by his side. He found the dressings, extracted them and then turned on his heel.

Holly stirred momentarily as he picked one foot up and then sighed in her sleep as he gently dressed her wounds. Blisters in such a moist, bacteria-rich environment could be a real problem, turning very nasty very quickly. The dressings he applied protected and cushioned them.

He replaced her feet back on the ground and watched as she turned on her side. Asleep she looked younger. Barely twenty. He shook his head and deliberately turned away so his back was to her and watched the camp activity through the wooden slats of their jail. He memorised every detail, knowing that he would be debriefed once they got back and any intelligence he could relay would be helpful. And he really needed to concentrate on something else!

He saw John approach an hour later and he rose to his feet and faced the door as it swung open, not wanting to wake Holly.

'We need you. One of our children has malaria, she's not doing very well,' said John.

Richard knew because malaria was his field that the young were hit hardest by this disease and that worldwide infant mortality from it was frighteningly high. Cerebral malaria, which was fatal, was too often a progression of the disease mostly seen in children.

He entered the darkened shelter and pushed through a small group of women who were huddled around a low bed. The baby, a girl, was lying naked and very still, and Richard noted her pallor despite the poor lighting.

He knelt beside the sick child and felt for a pulse. A commotion broke out around him. The elderly woman who had been holding the little girl's hand pushed at him and jabbered loudly, lifting the girl into her arms away from Richard's touch. She rocked the baby and her cries bordered on wailing. The other women joined in and Richard stood and looked enquiringly at John.

'What's wrong?' he asked. 'The girl is very sick, I need to examine her.' Richard tried to keep the alarm at the baby's condition out of his voice but even a cursory glance had told him she was severely dehydrated.

'Tuti's grandmother doesn't want a man. It is an old custom, not practised much any more. Girls are to be doctored to only by other women until they are married. I didn't think the old woman would be too fussy given the condition of the child.'

Having worked in many areas where local customs were sacrosanct, Richard appreciated the situation. But it was frustrating nonetheless. 'Where is the mother?' Richard asked.

'She was a victim of the typhoon. Mundi has cared for Tuti ever since.'

Richard's mind raced. They were wasting valuable time. He needed to rehydrate the baby and get her medical attention.

'Get Holly,' he said to Richard. She could be his eyes and his hands.

Holly was dragged out of a deep sleep by determined shaking. A rebel soldier, gun slung over his shoulder, was prodding her arm and jabbering insistently at her. She looked around for Richard, feeling frightened, but as he pulled at her arm it seemed he just wanted her to follow him.

She accompanied him, her heart banging in her rib cage. What had happened? What did he want? Where was Richard? The soldier hurried through the centre of the camp, startling chickens and children in his wake.

They entered a very noisy, crowded shelter and she almost sagged in relief when she saw Richard. There was a low, deep, anguished sound reverberating through the crowd of women and Holly got goose-bumps. It sounded mournful and her skin prickled with apprehension this time. Had somebody died?

'Holly, I need you,' he said curtly, grabbing her by the arms. 'We have a very sick baby on our hands. As a man, I'm not allowed to treat her. You're going to have to do it for me. Are you up for it? She's going to die if we don't get fluids into her.'

Holly didn't hesitate. 'Of course.' She was a nurse after all.

'John, I want all of these women out,' said Richard. 'Mundi can stay but I want everyone else to leave.'

John cleared the shelter. The women were reluctant but John's authority appeared absolute.

Holly knelt beside Mundi and assessed the baby. She spoke her findings out loud for Richard's benefit. She felt for the pulse and lost count it was so rapid. The baby was burning up, its eyes sunken, its lips dried and cracked. She felt the baby's fontanelle, noting how depressed it was. The baby was otherwise well nourished and Holly was thankful for small mercies. This little girl was going to need every ounce of her baby fat.

'How old is she?' Richard spoke to John.

'Ten months.'

'How long has she been sick?'

John spoke briefly with Mundi who was sponging her granddaughter's body. 'Her fever and chills started yesterday. She has also had vomiting and diarrhoea.'

'Has she bled from anywhere?' Richard asked.

More consulting with Mundi. 'No.'

'We have to get a line in, Holly. She's severely dehydrated. We'll give her twenty per kilo over an hour. I'll make up some ten per cent dextrose solution. Her blood-sugar level is probably dangerously low.'

Holly swallowed and tried not to laugh hysterically. Get a line in? Where? Big veins she could do. But little ones? Dehydrated ones at that? She quickly inspected the baby's arms and legs for signs of a vein. She was never going to succeed.

Richard got all the stuff ready for Holly while his brain ticked over. From the description of the symptoms it sounded like malaria. And as much as he despised John, at least he'd recognized an illness that was endemic among the people of Tanrami.

There was no way he could tell which of the four strains it was. All he could do was treat the physical symptoms and get her to Abeil, where she could have the proper treatment. He hoped he wasn't too late. He hoped Tuti wasn't in the stage of developing the life-threatening cerebral malaria and died before he could get her proper medical attention.

He watched Holly as he mixed some fifty per cent glucose with Hartman's solution to make the bag about a ten per cent dextrose mix. She was having difficulty finding a vein.

'Try the scalp,' he said, a needle cap between his teeth as he pushed the sugary solution into the bag of fluid.

His mind moved on. Weight.

'How much does she weigh, do you reckon?' he asked Holly. He figured as a midwife she'd be pretty good at guessing babies' weights.

Holly assessed the infant, trying to make an educated estimate. Not very much. 'About seven kilos…maybe?'

He nodded and filled the burette up with one hundred and forty mils of fluid. Holly could run it in over an hour once she got the drip in.

Holly inspected the scalp and mumbled thanks to Mundi, who drew a lantern nearer. Luckily the baby was bald so the veins were easier to identify. Or they would have been had there been any! There was nothing. Tuti was just too dehydrated.

'Forget it,' said Richard, handing her an intra-osseous needle. 'Use this. We don't have time.'

Holly looked at the rather brutal instrument. He was right. It was the quickest and easiest way for them to administer fluids, but she'd never placed one before, although she had seen it done and understood the theory.

The needle was basically a fancy screw that was twisted into the bone, accessing the bone marrow and using it to deliver fluid and medications.

She shut her eyes and sent a little plea out into the ether. 'Tibia?' she asked.

'Just below the knee, in the broadest, flattest part of the bone.' He nodded at her encouragingly.

Her hand shook as she grasped the large knob, positioned the needle so the tip pointed away from the joint space and pushed down firmly, twisting the knob in a screwing motion. She gritted her teeth as the sharp inner trocar ground through the bone. The baby didn't flinch, cry or move.

She felt a gentle give as the soft layer of bone marrow was breached and breathed a sigh of relief. The needle stood upright unsupported in the bone.

'Well done, Holly,' said Richard. It had been a tricky procedure, and she had managed it better than a lot of doctors he had seen. And Tuti couldn't have afforded her to fail.

Holy grinned at him, warmed by his compliment, and was surprised by his answering smile. It was a hundred-watt dazzler! He'd obviously been holding his breath too.

Richard passed her a dressing as she removed the central trocar. She secured the site and hooked up the IV line, adjusting the roller clamp to deliver the fluid in the burette over an hour.

'We need to evacuate her,' Richard said, turning to John, who was watching them dispassionately.

'No.'

'She needs hospitalisation. If it's malaria then it needs to be treated or she could die.'

'Many of our children die, Sergeant. What do you care?'

'I care about this child. I'm not going to stand by and watch her die from a totally curable illness.'

'She is a girl.' He shrugged.

Holly felt her ire rise and turned from her observation of the baby. She remembered Richard's warning to keep her mouth shut, but this was really too much! She wouldn't be silent in the face of such blatant discrimination.

'She is a human being. She has as much right to live and to medical care as the next child.' Holly's chest heaved as she swallowed her fear and confronted John.

'She can't fight and she's too young to work. She is just another mouth to feed,' John dismissed.

The coldness of his statement put a chill right up her spine. 'I didn't think the rebels were so primitive,' said Holly, rising to her feet, pulling herself up to her full five feet two and giving him a look of sheer disgust. 'Richard has been telling me you lot are dangerous and not to be trusted. I've been telling him he's wrong. Is he right, John? Are you just a band of barbaric savages or are you noble mountain people with a just cause?'

Holly's heart was hammering. She couldn't sit by and let him dismiss this child's life as worthless because of her sex.

Richard blinked at her outburst. She might be a woman but at the moment she was an angry one and she wasn't taking any prisoners. He stifled the caution that sprang to his lips. Maybe she could shame John into action.

Mundi let out a cry and Holly and Richard turned in time to see Tuti convulsing.

'Get her on her side,' Richard ordered.

'Yes, I do know that,' Holly snapped. She hadn't meant to sound so terse but her run-in with John had made her irritable.

Holly flipped Tuti on her side and waited for the jerking of her limbs to stop. Mundi sobbed and wailed and clutched at Holly's shirt. The old woman spoke to her with anguished eyes. Holly didn't know the words but the meaning was clear. Do something. Help her.

'Do you think it's related to her fever or a worsening of the malaria?' Holly asked Richard as the convulsions began to subside.

GET FREE BOOKS and a FREE MYSTERY GIFT WHEN YOU PLAY THE...

SLOT MACHINE GAME!

Just scratch off the silver box with a coin. Then check below to see the gifts you get!

YES! I have scratched off the silver box. Please send me the four FREE books and mystery gift for which I qualify. I understand I am under no obligation to purchase any books, as explained on the back of this card. I am over 18 years of age.

Mrs/Miss/Ms/Mr _____ Initials _____   **M6EI**

BLOCK CAPITALS PLEASE

Surname _____

Address _____

_____

Postcode _____

7	7	7	Worth FOUR FREE BOOKS plus a BONUS Mystery Gift!
🍒	🍒	🍒	Worth FOUR FREE BOOKS!
♣	♣	♣	Worth ONE FREE BOOK!
🔔	🔔	🍒	TRY AGAIN!

Visit us online at www.millsandboon.co.uk

Offer valid in the U.K. only and is not available to current Reader Service subscribers to this series. Overseas and Eire please write for details. We reserve the right to refuse an application and applicants must be aged 18 years or over. Offer expires 31st July 2006. Terms and prices subject to change without notice. As a result of this application you may receive further offers from carefully selected companies. If you do not wish to share in this opportunity, please write to the Data Manager at the address shown overleaf. Only one application per household.

Mills & Boon® is a registered trademark owned by Harlequin Mills & Boon Limited.

Reader Service™ is being used as a trademark.

The Reader Service™ — Here's how it works:

Accepting the free books places you under no obligation to buy anything. You may keep the books and gift and return the despatch note marked 'cancel'. If we do not hear from you, about a month later we'll send you 6 brand new books and invoice you just £2.80* each. That's the complete price - there is no extra charge for postage and packing. You may cancel at any time, otherwise every month we'll send you 6 more books, which you may either purchase or return to us - the choice is yours.

*Terms and prices subject to change without notice.

NO STAMP NEEDED!

THE READER SERVICE™
FREE BOOK OFFER
FREEPOST CN81
CROYDON
CR9 3WZ

NO STAMP
NECESSARY
IF POSTED IN
THE U.K. OR N.I.

'It could be either,' he said, running his hands through his short hair. It was hot in the shelter and he felt a fine sheen of sweat lining his scalp. He couldn't be certain without vital tests. Tuti needed urgent hospitalisation.

'Well.' Holly turned and glared at John. 'Are you going to prove him wrong,' she pointed at Richard, 'and do the right thing?'

Richard held his breath. Holly's goading had hit the mark. John's face was puce with barely concealed rage. Richard hoped that Holly hadn't gone too far.

'She needs to go to Abeil,' Richard said, keeping up the pressure and trying to keep his frustration in check.

John nodded curtly and stalked out of the shelter. Tuti's limbs had stilled and Holly encouraged Mundi to sponge her grandaughter down. Richard followed John out.

John appeared to be organising an evacuation. Two soldiers scurried away and came back a few minutes later with a small stretcher.

'Let Holly go with them,' he said, interrupting the conversation between John and his men.

'I give the orders here,' John snapped, ignoring Richard's presence.

'Tuti needs a medical escort,' Richard persisted.

'Holly stays. You stay. Tuti and Mundi will go to Abeil as soon as you clear them to move.'

'It will take too long on foot. We could get a chopper from the field hospital—'

John pulled Richard's pistol out, cocked it and pointed it at Richard's head. 'They go by foot or not at all. Do not test my patience any further.'

Richard withdrew. He walked back into the shelter seething inwardly.

'How is she?' he asked Holly, and dredged up a reassuring smile.

'The same. Maybe a little less tachycardic. The bolus is almost finished. What's happening? Are they moving her?'

'Yep. Organising it now.' he nodded.

Holly smiled triumphantly, her spirits and hopes for little Tuti lifting dramatically. 'See, Richard, I told you. They're just misunderstood. It's going to be OK.'

Richard nodded again. She looked so happy, so righteous, he didn't have the heart to dash it all. She had had her first real glimpse of the disregard that John and his type had for human life and had managed to put a positive spin on it. He hoped she never got to see it as it really was.

Because it was ugly.

CHAPTER SEVEN

RICHARD slept. Two days of hard marching and only brief episodes of dozing the night before was a potent sleeping pill. The stress levels that had soared through his system, working on the dehydrated infant and their abduction and the subsequent worry about Holly's safety had left his tough-guy reserves seriously depleted.

He also knew that tomorrow was going to be his biggest challenge. Tomorrow he had to treat the rebel leader and earn their freedom. A million scenarios had circled through his head as he had reclined on the dirt floor of their prison and he had pushed them all aside to allow sleep to claim him instead. He was going to have to be alert. Their lives would depend on it.

Perversely, Holly couldn't sleep. She lay awake watching the steady rise and fall of Richard's chest as the firelight cast fingers of orange light across his body. She still quaked a little when she thought about her angry words with John but the result had been worth it. They had helped another person on their travels.

She shivered when she thought about how ill the little girl was. The fear she had see in Mundi's eyes and the desperation in her voice would stay with her for ever. So would the callousness of John. Had she been wrong about the rebels? No, when it mattered, John had done the decent thing. The honourable thing.

Richard mumbled in his sleep and her gaze rested on him

again. Her eyes caressed his features. His strong jawline was heavy with dark stubble, his short black hair peppered with grey and his lips slackened by slumber. In fact, the whole harshness of his face had disappeared, the severity of his features relaxed now.

It was great to be able to stare at him for a change. Two days of him following her had made her very conscious of her appearance despite their dire situation. When she had bought the cargos just prior to her departure from Australia she hadn't thought she'd be trekking through a jungle with an ex-lover behind her. If she had, she might have been more critical of how her butt looked in them.

Mind you, it probably didn't matter at this point. Every part of her must have looked like something the cat had dragged in. With no mirror to confirm her worst suspicions, she just had to guess. After two days without soap or toothpaste, she was more *au naturel* than she had ever wanted to be.

Still, she thought as sleep started to muddle her brain, at least she was clean—intermittent dousing with torrential rain saw to that. And didn't they say rainwater was good for your skin? Whatever. She'd kill for some soap and the opportunity to get naked and wash herself all over. Some shampoo and even a little moisturiser wouldn't go astray either.

And she only had four sticks of gum left in her pocket, which she had been sharing with Richard. Even if it didn't do much for oral hygiene, at least her mouth felt refreshed and her breath didn't smell like birdcage effluent. But, oh, if she ever got out of this alive, she was going to sit in a spa bath all day and pamper herself.

A couple of hours later she was dreaming about precisely that when a sudden shout woke her. She sat bolt upright, her muscles protesting the quick movement, disorientated at first. The fire had burned low, just a few coals glowing in the stone ring, and she heard the unmistakable sound of thunder and rain beating down outside.

Her heart rate settled as she realised the noise had come from outside and she glanced over at Richard to tell him it was just thunder. But he was asleep. Strange, very strange. Surely tough-guy, action-figure Richard would be instantly alert at a noise that had managed to drag her awake?

Nothing woke her. She was a shift worker. Her family called her log. As in sleeping-like-a. But Richard? Weren't professional soldiers supposed to sleep with one eye open or something? Weren't they supposed to be instantly alert if so much as a leaf crunched?

Then she noticed the sweat beading his brow and then he muttered in his sleep again and shook his head from side to side.

'No,' he shouted, and Holly nearly jumped out of her skin. That had been the noise that had woken her. It hadn't been thunder. It had been Richard. She watched as he muttered again and she saw the rapid movements of his eyes beneath his closed lids and guessed he was dreaming. Bad dreaming.

'No,' he shouted again, and she watched as his fingers curled into fists.

OK. What was she supposed to do now? The rain continued to thunder down outside so she doubted anyone in the camp had heard him. Did she just leave him and hope that he would wake of his own accord, or was she supposed to rouse him? The look on his face, twisted in agony, was too awful to bear. What was he dreaming about?

Her urge was to go to him and hold him. Whatever he was dreaming about, it was bad. He looked in so much pain, so alone. Maybe even if only his subconscious knew she was beside him, it might help him feel less alone.

She shuffled over and sat nearer. She reached for a log and threw it on the fire, poking at the coals with a stick to stir them up. She watched him a bit longer as he muttered to himself, still undecided.

And then he started to whimper. He sounded like a wounded

animal. It was such an anguished sound her heart squeezed painfully in her chest. She couldn't stand to listen to it any more. She lay on her side next to him, propped up on one elbow.

'Richard,' she whispered, and placed her hand on his firmly muscled chest. 'Richard.'

He either didn't hear her or couldn't wake from the bounds of his dream. She tried again, shaking him a little more firmly this time. Still nothing. And still a gut-wrenching whimpering that clawed at her soul.

Holly got down closer to his ear and whispered again. His head shook from side to side and she gently kissed the side of his face, close to his ear. 'Richard, it's OK. Wake up,' she said, and kissed him lightly again in the same spot.

She couldn't explain why she'd decided to kiss him. In fact, it hadn't even been a conscious decision. It had just happened on the spur of the moment. It hadn't even been sexual. Just one person trying to comfort another, a bit like a mother trying to soothe a frightened child. Because that's exactly what Richard looked like—a scared little boy.

'Richard,' she said again, kissing his sweaty brow. 'Richard.' This time she kissed a closed eyelid. 'Wake up, you're dreaming. It's OK, it's Holly. Wake up.'

She continued to whisper words of comfort and solace to him as she dropped gentle kisses all over his face. His fretting eased and she stroked her fingers through his hair and across his forehead. His face, contorted with a mix of emotions, relaxed and Holly snuggled her head against his chest and listened to the reassuring thud of his heart beating.

A few minutes later the head-shaking and muttering started again and Holly was quick to repeat her earlier ministrations.

'It's OK Richard. I'm with you. Holly's here. It's OK.'

Richard's eyes snapped open and the orange glow cast around the small area made them look even blacker. He looked at her, confusion evident in their dark depths. He didn't look fully awake to her so she kept whispering, telling him he was OK and that she was there for him. And it seemed like the most natural thing in the world to keep kissing him, dropping light kisses all over his face.

More importantly, he didn't even try to stop her. She stopped when he seemed more awake, his black eyes boring into hers, and laid her head back down on his chest for a while. His arm came up around her shoulders, scooping her closer, and she sighed and relaxed against him.

'You had a bad dream,' she said quietly. His heartbeat had steadied and the sound and feel of it beneath her ear seemed as natural as the rain beating down around them.

'Yes,' he said. 'I'm sorry. I didn't mean to wake you.'

Holly raised herself on her elbow. 'Don't be ridiculous, Richard. We can't control our subconscious.'

'I can,' he said, removing his arm from around her and putting it by his side between them.

Holly sighed. Now he was going to be a he-man about this? He seriously needed to open up a bit more. 'Tell me about it,' she said, lying back down on her side beside him, an arm propped beneath her head as a pillow, her body not quite touching his.

'It's not important,' he said.

'It is to me.'

'Why?'

'I want to be able to understand you. And because…you woke me.' She smiled. 'And it wouldn't be fair to do that and not explain.'

He gave her a half-smile back. 'Life, my dear Pollyanna, isn't fair.' And he promptly turned his back on her.

'Was it a premonition? Was it about us being killed?'

'No.'

'Being rescued?'

'Nope.'

'Your childhood?'

'Holly. Go to sleep.'

'Nope,' she mimicked.

Silence.

'Mosquitoes?'

Silence.

'Giant mosquitoes?'

More silence. She cast around for something else. She was getting kind of desperate now. 'Monsters?'

Richard flinched and squeezed his eyes shut. Now she was getting closer. He still felt the tempo of his heartbeat pounding through every cell in his body and the familiar nausea that the dream always caused rolled through his gut. He started counting to himself. Anything to divert his thoughts.

Twelve, thirteen, fourteen—

'Some other evil force that big tough guys are scared of?'

Why didn't she just shut the hell up? Fifteen, sixteen, seventeen—

'Please, Richard,' she said, unable to keep the pleading tone from her voice, 'talk to me.'

'Go to sleep, Holly,' he said gruffly.

'No. I'm going to guess all night. You may as well just tell me.'

Richard sighed. Unfortunately he believed her.

'Holly, enough,' he said, turning over to his other side so he was facing her.

'Please, Richard,' she whispered.

He shut his eyes. What the hell? If it meant that much to her and she'd actually be quiet, it'd have to be worth it.

'It was about the thing that I told you about today.'

'What? The Africa thing?'

'Yes.'

Holly held her breath. She felt like one false move, one wrong word would send him scuttling in retreat. 'What happened?'

'I killed someone.'

His bluntness pulled her up. His shuttered face was illuminated by the firelight and she could see the anguish etched there.

Think, dammit, think. 'You were a soldier in a war zone,' she said quietly, quelling the urge to stroke his face. 'I guess sometimes that happens? Right?'

'Wrong. I was part of a United Nations mission. Your weapon is to be used only if there is an immediate threat to your life.'

'And there wasn't?'

'Not to mine, no.' He grimaced as he remembered that day. 'I mean, how crazy is that? They can shoot someone, an innocent civilian, right in front of your eyes and you can't do a damn thing about it.'

'Is that what happened?' she asked softly. There was silence for a while and she watched as his eyes returned from a faraway place and came back to focus on her.

He nodded. 'I came across this rebel soldier on the outskirts of the camp who had rounded up a woman with two children. One was a baby and the other was probably no more than two. He was trying to prise the toddler away from her leg and she was screaming and crying and begging him to leave them alone.'

'Oh, Richard, how awful.'

'It became apparent he was making her decide. Forcing her to choose which child lived and which child died. He was so cocky. So...damn sure of himself. He knew I couldn't do a damn thing about it.'

'But you did.'

'Well, I wasn't just going to stand by and let him do that. So I intervened. I took out my rifle, pointed it at his head and...he laughed at me. He was only about nineteen or twenty but he was cold. Worse than cold. There was this maniacal, zealous glint in his eyes. He was so indoctrinated he couldn't see that an innocent woman and her children had no part in his stupid war. And he was getting such a sadistic kick out of terrorising her…' Richard shuddered as the chill that had swept through his bones that day revisited him.

Holly stayed silent. She could feel the tears welling in her eyes and goose-bumps prickle her skin at the eeriness of his tone. He had left her. She could tell he was back reliving that day.

'And then he grabbed the baby out of her arms and the mother was sobbing and wailing and begging him. She threw herself at his feet and clutched at his clothes and the toddler was screaming and he just laughed. This horrible, cold laugh. And even though I couldn't tell what she was saying, I could see she was offering herself instead. She kept pointing to her chest and trying to take the baby off him.'

Holly felt a tear leave her eyes and track its way down her cheek. 'So you shot him?'

Richard looked at her, her voice bringing him back to the present. He looked at her silently for a few seconds. 'No. Not then. I pressed the weapon to his head and demanded he give the baby back. And then…'

She watched the play of emotions on his face and gave him some breathing space. 'Then?'

'He sneered at me, took a step back, threw the baby in the air and while we all looked up he started to pepper the air with automatic gunfire…and I shot him. One bullet, straight through the heart. He dropped instantly.'

Holly bit back a sob as Richard's face blurred before her. She couldn't even begin to imagine the horror of what he'd just described. 'The baby?'

'The baby landed on the ground before any of us had a chance to catch it. He had taken a hit to his leg. I scooped him out of the dirt, picked the mother and the other child up and ran with them back to the casualty station. He was evacuated immediately. He survived.'

She saw the lines of strain around his mouth and eyes that retelling the story had caused. She touched his face with tentative fingers, stroking the deep furrows on his forehead. 'I'm so sorry, Richard,' she whispered. 'What an awful, awful thing to have been through.' She stroked his temples. 'What a terrible nightmare.'

Richard closed his eyes as her touch caressed his face. It was nice and he felt the tangible sense of dread recede. 'That's not the worst part of the dream,' he said, opening his eyes. What the hell? She may as well know it all.

'Oh?'

'It starts off with me witnessing an argument between my parents when I was a kid, about ten. My father starts to beat my mother and I'm crying and yelling for him to stop, and then suddenly the scene morphs into the baby incident, but I'm still ten and the soldier is ignoring me and I'm still helpless to stop it. Just as helpless as I always was at home.'

Holly heard the anguish in his voice. 'Hush,' she whispered, placing her fingers on his lips. 'You were a child, Richard. What could you do?'

'Something. Anything. I shouldn't have just let him beat her.'

His lips moved against her fingers and her heart filled with compassion. She tried to picture Richard as a frightened ten-year-old and failed. He seemed so capable. So sure of himself. But she could see the child in his eyes and she wanted to lend him some comfort.

Holly leaned forward and placed a gentle kiss against his passive lips. She pulled back slightly and saw the wariness creep into his black eyes. 'It's OK, Richard,' she said quietly, because he looked like he was going to bolt at any second. 'Just relax, it's OK.' She kissed the corner of his mouth this time. 'Tell me more about it. Were you scared…that day with the soldier?'

'Terrified,' he admitted, accepting another light kiss on his lips, feeling parts of his body stir to life. 'But I think I was angry…more than anything. Everywhere we looked there were such dreadful human rights violations and we were unable to do anything. There was this overwhelming feeling of impotence denting our morale. And when I saw him tormenting that mother…I think I just snapped. They reminded me so much of me. Alone and defenceless with no one to stick up for them. I was scared, yes, but primarily I was just pissed off.'

No wonder he was so screwed up, she thought as she listened to his story. She kissed him again on the lips and this time he kissed her back, their lips holding for a brief moment.

He felt her lips at his temple and then his ear. It was getting harder to remember that acute sense of impotence now. Holly's kisses were making him feel anything but.

'What I don't understand is why it destroyed your chance of promotion. The way I look at it, you were a hero that day.' And she kissed him full on the mouth to try and convey her belief. The world needed men like Richard. Noble men, ready to defend the weak and the downtrodden. She broke away, slightly out of breath to finish what she wanted to say before she forgot how to speak. 'They should have given you a medal for bravery.'

Her lips were moist from their kissing and mere millimetres from his. It was such a Pollyanna thing to say he kissed her again. It must be nice to live in her world, he thought as she moaned against his mouth, where everything was so simple, so clear-cut. Unfortunately UN conventions weren't so black and white. But to have someone so totally in his corner was a turn-on nonetheless.

'The justification doesn't matter. My life wasn't at risk,' his voice was husky against her mouth, 'I was reported and disciplined.'

'Do you regret it?' she asked.

'No,' he said, and gave her a brief hard kiss. 'I don't. If I had my time over again I'd probably do the same thing. You see, it was instinctive, pulling the trigger, there was nothing conscious about it. I had to stop him shooting at the baby. But killing another human being, no matter what the provocation, diminishes you, and realistically I didn't have to shoot to kill.'

She looked at the self-doubt in his eyes and for the second time in her life she fell in love with him. His heroic actions hadn't brought him any triumph. He'd saved a life but taken another in its place, and it had obviously taken a piece out of him.

She felt his conflict. How awful to have to make a decision in a split second when emotions were running high and a life was at stake. And to spend years with it on your conscience, trying to rationalise it and stop the nightmares. He was truly an honourable man.

He could have killed without conscience, without batting an eyelid, but it was the measure of the type of man he was that his actions had caused him much angst. Love surged through her, a stronger, more mature love than she had ever felt. Richard had changed and so had she. But one thing hadn't— Richard, her damaged hero, needed her love more than ever.

And there was nothing light or feathery about her kiss this time. She unleashed herself, pouring all her love and the pride she felt at his actions into the kiss. She moved closer so their bodies were touching, trying to imprint herself upon him, convey the depth of her feelings.

Richard reeled from the kiss, grabbing hold of her hip, almost drowning in the surge of need that swamped him. He held her face and joined in the mutual raging desire. His tongue plunged into her mouth and hers met his with equal power. He wanted her, there was still something between them that was useless to deny. He must have her.

Holly's heart sang. This. This thing between them had never gone away. She'd spent two years telling herself she didn't love him any more, but now she knew this passion and strength of feeling could never just be over. And he could deny it all he wanted but she could feel it emanating from every cell in his body, too.

She wanted him inside her so badly that kissing was exquisite torture. She didn't care that their circumstances were less than the best. If she was going to die tomorrow or some time in the next few days then she wanted to go knowing that for a brief while he had loved her. She could feel his hardness pressing into her belly and gave in to the urge to touch it.

Richard almost jumped at the unexpected intimate pressure on his erection as Holly fondled him. It brought him back to earth with a thump. Whoa, there! This was getting a little out of control. When had a spot of kissing become so serious? They were in a jungle, for heaven's sake, with armed guards outside their door!

He broke away from her mouth and she opened her eyes and looked at him questioningly.

'Richard?' She frowned.

Her voice was husky and her lips were swollen from their passion and her eyes had that glazed, drunk kind of look and he very nearly kissed her again.

'We can't do this, Holly,' he said, drawing in deep ragged breaths. He couldn't protect her properly if their relationship became intimate. It would be too distracting and he couldn't afford any lapse in concentration. It was important to stay aloof from her and focused on his mission. Saving Fumradi and gaining their release.

He sat up, distancing himself from her stunned stare. He could see her trying to get her head around what he was saying and not quite believing the words.

'Of course,' she said, shutting her eyes, already wishing she had the last few moments back not to have made such a fool of herself. But part of her wanted to cry out, Why not? If they were going to die soon, why not go out on a sexual high?

'I'm sorry,' he said, his breathing now under control. 'I shouldn't have let you kiss me.'

'No, I'm sorry. I was just trying to…comfort you. Your

nightmare…I wanted to help you forget.' It wasn't a total lie but she had to say it lest she told him the truth. A truth he wasn't ready to hear. Maybe never would be. That she wanted him and needed him and loved him in every way a woman could love a man.

Unfortunately their situation was complex to say the least. There were still too many of those barriers he'd put up in his mind for their relationship to blossom into something deeper. And particularly while they were still prisoners, she knew there was no way he was ever going to accept her feelings. That she knew for certain. He needed to be the big tough guy and focus, and he didn't want silly, girly admissions distracting him.

'Thanks,' he said, his back still to her. 'I don't need any help.'

'Yeah, I got that,' she said, and turned on her side away from him.

Holly slept badly for the remainder of the night. She relived the kissing in her mind over and over. It didn't help that he was so close. Her fingers itched to touch him as each wave of hot desire surged through her belly. She pressed a fist between her thighs and clamped her legs shut tight to stop the tingling sensation burning down there. She almost wished it was morning and she was marching up the mountain again.

Fortunately morning came soon enough and neither of them were in a talking mood as they ate their cold rice. Richard wanted to apologise again but felt it was probably better to just forget it had ever happened. She appeared to be giving him the silent treatment anyway. It didn't matter. Today was too important to their survival to worry about whether she liked him or not. It wasn't high school. This unfortunately was as real and harsh as life got.

'Come now,' said John as he opened their door. 'Today is the day you fulfil your purpose.'

Holly was pleasantly surprised to find that her muscle pain

had lessened. They were still sore but the excruciating agony of every step had eased considerably. She must be getting used to the punishing climb, she thought, and then grimaced at the sobering thought.

They moved out in their usual formation. Richard chose to zone out the sway of Holly's bottom by centering his mind on the challenges of the day. Fumradi had a bullet wound. It sounded infected. He'd need to probe the wound for any retained particles, clean it, administer some antibiotics and replace his fluid loss.

He knew he could do those things with his kit, easy. Should Fumradi require more intensive care, then they were probably toast. He'd know more when he laid eyes on his patient. For the moment all he had was an educated guess.

Holly put one foot in front of the other, mulling over the conundrum that was Richard to take her mind off the endless trek upwards. She'd learned another piece of the puzzle last night and shuddered as goose-bumps broke out on her skin despite the oppressively hot conditions. Richard had seen man's inhumanity to man up close and personal. That had to screw you up a little.

She hadn't really appreciated how complex he was until last night. She was no longer just dealing with his crappy childhood or his failed engagement to a younger woman but an incident of terrible human cruelty. It had hardened him and made him seem so much more unreachable than he had ever been before.

They walked for hours, the choppers of the day before nowhere in sight today. Holly's legs felt much better but two days of marching and not much sustenance was really testing her stamina. Exhaustion never seemed very far away.

Even the thought that they'd soon reach their destination wasn't enough to lift her mood. Yes, the endless walking would at last be over but she knew that their fate awaited them at the top and perversely she wished the mountain would stretch upwards for ever.

Holly smelt the woodsmoke long before the camp came into sight. As they neared, a young boy wandered down the track towards them and greeted the soldiers. He looked about five or six but given his state of malnutrition he could well have been older. His large protruding stomach stuck out from his ill-fitting ragged T-shirt and his skinny arms and legs didn't look strong enough to support even his feather-light weight.

He eyed them curiously but said nothing. He had large brown eyes, light brown skin and that solemn look she'd seen on so many children's faces since she'd been in Tanrami. His long dark hair looked unkempt, the fringe almost blinding him and the back brushing his shoulders.

The soldiers at the front of the procession unloaded their backpacks and gave them to the boy. She gasped as he uncomplainingly hitched them on his shoulders. His limbs looked like they'd snap under the extra weight and Holly swore she saw him sink a few centimetres shorter.

Her heart went out to him as she watched him struggle with his load. The men appeared to be finding his efforts funny. How could grown men burden such a small child with man-sized baggage?

She felt hot acid rise and burn in her chest. For the first time since their ordeal had begun, the total of all the despicable things she had seen hit her hard. She was beginning to feel real contempt for the rebels. Until now, despite everything, she'd still felt tremendous sympathy for their plight. But now there was just disdain.

Richard brushed past her and she wondered what he was doing. When he walked past the two soldiers ahead they tried to restrain him but he shrugged them off. He reached the young boy and placed a hand on one of the backpacks, stopping the boy in his tracks. He unloaded the child and shouldered the packs himself.

John brushed past her next and Holly kicked on some speed.

'Give the packs to the child. It is Tundol's job,' said John, barring Richard's ascent.

'You use a child to do a man's work?'

John's face hardened. 'He likes it. He is grateful to the freedom fighters.'

'What do you mean?' asked Holly from behind as she caught the conversation. She watched the child, who stood quietly regarding the adults' conversation solemnly.

'We found him in Abeil, scavenging for food. He was displaced during the typhoon. His family, his village are all dead.'

'He's an orphan?' she asked incredulously.

'Yes,' confirmed John. He flicked ash from the end of his cigarette in Tundol's direction.

'And you use him as a slave?' Richard's voice left no one in any doubt of his contempt.

'He earns his keep.' John bristled.

'As a packhorse? A mule?' demanded Richard.

'He is strong.' John shrugged dismissively.

'He's a boy,' Holly hissed. She felt hot tears scald her eyes at their callousness.

She looked at him and Richard saw her utter disbelief and disillusionment that people she had defended could do such a thing. She looked totally crushed and his heart went out to her. Shattered ideals were always hard to deal with.

John looked down at the sad-looking child with big, brown eyes and gave a curt order. He scampered up the track but not before Holly saw fear in the child's eyes. What had the poor boy been forced to do since the typhoon had separated him from his family?

'You want to carry Tundol's load, be my guest, Sergeant. But hurry. Fumradi waits for you.'

They fell back into line and arrived in the camp about ten minutes later. Holly was still too angry to fully appreciate the surroundings. Top camp was luxurious compared to the rudimentary dwellings of the lower camps. An impressive large abode dominated the area. It reminded Holly of the treehouse in the movie *Swiss Family Robinson,* which she had seen as a child.

It was made of timber and nestled in the thick canopy, high above the forest floor. The other living quarters weren't as big but were also elevated off the ground and a series of wooden bridges connected each to the other. It looked kind of surreal, like a magical forest kingdom.

Holly noticed Tundol as soon as they entered the camp. He was sitting alone near the sturdy animal pens, while a band of other children played happily together nearby. He looked so sad and alone and isolated.

The soldiers were greeted by a throng of locals, as they had been previously, and Holly took the opportunity to talk to Richard.

'I'm not leaving this camp without Tundol,' she whispered, placing her hand on his arm.

Richard looked at her and something inside him shifted. He recognised a kindred spirit and placed his hand over hers. She had seen an injustice perpetrated on an innocent child and had decided to make a stand. To look out for him, to defend him. And he, probably more than most people, understood how she felt.

Tundol's treatment had appalled him also, but he suspected that John probably wouldn't give the boy up easily. Maybe if they managed to cure the ailing rebel leader, they would have a good bargaining chip. If they didn't, and had to run?

A child would seriously hinder their progress. He glanced over at the boy and Tundol looked directly at him. Richard looked back at Holly and saw the purpose in her eyes.

'I don't want to leave him either, Holly, but it's too risky.'

'We can't leave him here with these, these…' She cast around for a suitable description. Something that would convey her utter disgust at their treatment of Tundol.

'Poor, misunderstood freedom fighters?'

She glared at him mutinously. How dared he throw that back in her face? So, she may have been wrong about these people. Did he have to rub it in? Her body was broken, her spirit was crushed. Wasn't she already defeated enough?

'Animals,' she hissed back at him, and couldn't even muster sorrow that her idealistic fantasy had been shattered in a million pieces.

'Come,' John interrupted, and signalled them to follow. 'There is work to be done.'

Richard felt his heart start to beat louder as they followed John up some steep wooden steps into the large home of the rebel leader. The house had looked big from the outside but the reality was even more impressive.

'Wait here,' said John at a doorway. He opened it and shut it behind him.

Holly felt…trepidation. What would they find behind the door? Could they help? And what if they couldn't? What did that mean for them and for that poor orphan child outside? She glanced at Richard and he smiled at her reassuringly, but she could see the same doubts assailed him.

John opened the door. 'Fumradi is worse. It looks like we're just in time.'

Great, thought Richard. Maybe John should have abducted a magician. John stood aside and Richard's worst fears were confirmed. The rebel leader was propped up in bed by several pillows and looked very unwell.

Richard met the rebel's leader blank gaze and knew with dreadful clarity he was looking into the eyes of a dead man.

CHAPTER EIGHT

THE first thing Holly noticed was the stench. It drifted over to them and she had to suppress the urge to wretch. She noticed a bloodied bandage on his right thigh and thought that if Fumradi wasn't septic she'd eat her hat. The smell of a purulent wound was something you never forgot and the rebel leader reeked of it. Great! We're dead, thought Holly.

A woman hovering around the bed, holding a cloth and wiping her leader's brow, caught her attention and Holly could see the worry etched on the woman's face. And quite rightly, too. Fumradi's skin had a distinctive yellow tinge, indicating jaundice and therefore probably liver failure. She hoped Richard had a magic wand in his pack.

And then as she advanced into the room with Richard she saw something even more alarming. Fumradi's skeletal chest vibrated with each boom of his bounding heart. She didn't even have to touch him to count his pulse, she could do it from the end of the bed. His heart was working at an alarming pace. He looked flushed and his forehead was beaded with sweat.

Richard knelt beside his patient and knew he couldn't save Fumradi. He doubted that even the high-tech medical care he'd get in a modern intensive care unit could have saved the rebel leader.

He was surprisingly young. Mid-twenties at most. 'Fumradi

is gravely ill,' he said, turning back to John. 'I cannot help him. He needs to be evacuated.'

'No evacuation.' John shook his head.

'He needs intensive care.'

'No hospital,' John reiterated.

'He's going to die,' said Richard, with barely concealed anger. 'Is that what you want? Are you going to tell those people out there that you let their leader die?'

'Best not let him die, then, Sergeant,' said John, his voice cold and hard.

Richard turned back, grinding his teeth together. He glanced at Holly on the other side of the bed and he could tell by the look on her face that her assessment of the situation was the same as his. Hopeless.

So, he thought. Fumradi would die. And that was going to be very bad for them. It was time to stop trying to change John's mind. He obviously wasn't going to budge. It was time to start thinking of ways to delay the man's death as long as possible and work out a way to escape.

'OK,' he said to Holly, quickly prioritising in his head the things they could offer him that could buy them some time. 'He needs fluids, antibiotics, his wound investigated and cleaned up. Let's get two IVs in and give him some colloid. We'll administer antibiotics and then we'll probe and clean his wound.'

Holly looked at him blankly. Surely he knew that Fumradi was still going to die, regardless of anything they did?

'I need my pack, John. Now.' Richard turned to see John disappearing out the door.

'Are you insane?' she hissed. 'He's at death's door and knocking really loudly. It doesn't matter what we do, he's still going to die.'

'Yes, I do realise that,' he replied quietly. 'I'm just trying to buy us some time.'

'For what?'

'To escape. You want to be here when they discover he's dead?'

'Of course not,' she said sarcastically. 'But how much time do you really think you can get us? If he's alive in an hour, I'll be amazed.'

Richard heard John's footsteps getting closer. 'He has to be, Holly. We need to get him through into the night. We're going to need the cover of darkness.'

Holly swallowed at the urgency of his tone. John handed the pack to Richard. It was three o'clock. Nightfall was sometime away yet. She glanced at Richard. He oozed confidence as he methodically pulled equipment from his pack. She couldn't help but compare him to the man she had kissed last night. He was gone. Only the machine remained.

He handed her an IV cannula. 'You get one in your side.' Maybe he could see the panic in her eyes because his hand lingered for a moment and he smiled at her encouragingly.

Holly's hand shook as she ripped open the packaging and assembled the tourniquet and other equipment she would need for when the needle slid into the vein.

Richard pierced his patient's skin, finding a vein immediately. Fumradi didn't flinch or protest at the sharp sting. 'John, can you ask her how long Fumradi has been unresponsive?' asked Richard, nodding to the woman who had been in the room when they had entered.

There was a brief exchange as Richard ran an IV line through. 'Since before lunch,' confirmed John.

Holly got a flashback and almost sagged in relief. Her hands were shaking so much she was sure she was going to stuff it up. 'When was the last time he passed urine?' Richard didn't look up from his task.

A further exchange. 'Yesterday.'

Holly glanced at Richard in alarm. Fumradi was in renal failure. His infected wound had obviously given him blood-borne septicaemia and had caused his kidneys to stop working. Untreated sepsis followed an ugly but predictable path, which usually led to multi-organ failure. His liver would be struggling too and his heart battling to keep it all together.

'OK,' said Richard, connecting the fluid to the cannula and jumping up from his squatting position. He opened the giving set up full bore. The two flasks of volume expander they were going to administer would help Fumradi's flagging circulation. And the triple antibiotics he was drawing up might temporarily knock the rapidly multiplying bacteria that were storming the man's system. He needed more than one dose but Richard didn't carry any more so it would have to do.

Holly hooked up her IV line and got it running. Richard handed her a syringe with an antibiotic in it, and she inserted the needle into the side port of the plastic line and pushed the drug into the drip. He did the same on the other side and as she watched the yellow fluid mix with the colloid solution, she crossed her fingers that it would buy them the time Richard was hoping for.

'Hold a mil back,' Richard said to her as he gave the last of the medication.

Holly didn't query him in front of an eagle-eyed John but she did look at him questioningly.

'I'll spray it into the wound,' he said. 'See if we can get a topical response.'

Holly blinked. OK, she'd never seen it done before with an intravenous preparation but Richard was the combat medicine expert. Or was he just clutching at straws?

'Shall we do the wound next?' Holly asked, changing her gloves.

'Yes,' he said, following suit.

Richard watched as Holly cut the dirty bandage away from their patient's thigh. He saw her nose wrinkle at the putrid smell and her shudder as the full extent of the infection was revealed. Pus oozed from the jagged wound that was about the size of an orange. Old clotted blood clung to the edges and the flesh looked dull and greyish. The stench intensified now the fabric barrier had been fully removed.

'Let's get it clean,' said Richard, straightening to remove himself from the potent aroma.

Holly sat back on her haunches, trying to mentally prepare herself. She was obviously going to have to work holding her breath. It was that or end up vomiting into the wound. Not that anything could make it any worse. The smell really was nauseating.

Richard pulled out a small sterile, single-use pack and opened it on the bed. There were two towels, several gauze squares, a small plastic bowl, a pair of long-necked forceps and a stitch holder. He filled the bowl with sterile saline and opened up some more gauze.

Holly turned her head and took a deep breath of relatively fresh air behind her, then moved reluctantly back towards the festering wound. She put the gauze into the bowl and watched as it soaked up the liquid. She picked up a square, squeezed out the excess saline and set about cleaning the wound.

The gauze glided across the rough surface of the deep wound, the tissue slippery beneath her fingers. As she discarded each piece of gauze she noted the greeny-yellow slime that coated them. Richard pushed around the edges of the wound, expressing pus that had become trapped in the jagged tissue.

Holly shifted away again, satisfied that the wound was as clean as she could get it, and sucked in some deep breaths of clean air. She watched Richard mix the remainder of the antibiotics together in one syringe and then add some saline to make the quantity up to ten mils.

Richard knew he was going to have to probe the wound. He didn't have the use of an X-ray machine to see if any shrapnel had been left behind. But he knew, given the amount of pus, that there had to be something still in there.

He put on another pair of gloves over the pair he was already wearing. Double gloving was essential for the procedure he was about to perform. It wasn't uncommon for foreign bodies such as shrapnel to cut through gloves. Two glove layers gave added protection in case the first glove was breeched.

He placed his latex-protected index finger into the wound, moving it around, pushing quite firmly, trying to locate any obvious retained fragments. Fumradi moaned slightly and Richard was surprised. Was the colloid having an effect already? The local woman tending the leader rushed to his side and mopped his brow again.

Richard thought he felt a large solid lump just below the surface in the centre of the wound. Ignoring the overpowering smell and his necessary proximity to it, Richard picked up the forceps. Not exactly the right tool for the job but they were all he had.

He inspected the wound closely and found a small opening in the bed of the wound. He pushed the forceps into it and probed around until the instrument hit the solid object. He closed his eyes as he manoeuvred the tips to grasp the foreign body. He wiggled it out slowly, encouraged by Fumradi's groans.

If he was responding to pain, their treatment was starting to have some effect. Richard knew it would only be a temporary rally, but it would give them some time and that was all he needed.

The offending object finally pulled free and Richard held it up to the light. A partial bullet fragment—no wonder the wound had been so full of pus, with this acting as a constant irritant. He dropped the metal object into the bowl with a dull thunk.

'Impossible,' said John. 'I told you, we got the bullet out.'

'Well, you left some behind,' said Richard, feeling a smugness he shouldn't have in the situation and a certain pleasure at John's loss of face.

'Let's dress it,' said Holly, jumping in as she felt the tension between the two men reaching a dangerous peak.

Richard broke his eye contact with John and got back to the task at hand. 'I'll just irrigate the wound with this,' he said to Holly as she prepared some soaked gauze. He squirted the antibiotic solution he had prepared earlier onto the surface of the wound and made sure he instilled it well into the area where the bullet fragment had lodged.

Holly grimaced as Fumradi protested the bite of the antibiotics on his raw, exposed flesh. She'd spilled enough antibiotics on paper cuts in her nursing career to know Richard's treatment would hurt like hell. When Richard had finished he placed a wad of wet gauze into the depression and Richard helped her bandage it in place.

He looked at her as she stuck tape to the bandage. She was holding up well under the pressure. He had no doubt that she knew the implications of failure. The fact they were going to fail was as immaterial as it was inevitable. They just had to do a convincing job.

Richard shuffled up closer to his patient's head. 'Fumradi,' he called in a firm voice. He shook the man's arm. 'Fumradi,' he repeated.

The man's eyes flicked the second time. Richard placed his thumbs beneath either eye and pulled down on the skin to expose the insides of the leader's bottom lids. He opened his mouth next and inspected the mucous membranes. He also picked up the leader's hands and inspected his nail beds.

Fumradi was desperately anaemic. Probably a combination of the blood Fumradi had lost through the initial wound to his leg and the septic process that chewed up red blood cells as quickly as they were made. The man needed a blood transfusion. Actually, he could do with several bags of blood but one could at least buy them some more time.

'He needs a transfusion,' said Richard.

Holly tried not to look at him like he'd grown a second head. A blood transfusion? Well, da, of course he did. She'd just go and check the blood fridge! 'Right? And we do that how?' she asked him quietly.

'I have the stuff in my kit but I'll need your help,' he said, and looked at her assessingly. She looked like she was only just managing to keep it together. But this was only the beginning. Later tonight he was going to ask so much more of her. If she baulked at this there was no way she'd be able to cope with being on the run. Being hunted. 'You up for it?'

Holly looked into his coal-black eyes and knew he wasn't just talking about the transfusion. Was she allowed to say no? That she was scared and she didn't want to die and that she loved him? But as she gazed into his eyes she saw his strength and his confidence and she knew that he needed her to have those things as well. That he'd get them out but she needed to put everything aside and concentrate on one thing only. Survival.

Holly felt her spine straighten. She'd do whatever was required of her to get the hell out of this godforsaken jungle and be able to tell Richard that she loved him. He wasn't going to accept it while they were still captive, so that was her goal. To get out, to survive, so she could start taking care of the man who stood before her. The tough-guy soldier with a bleeding heart and a damaged soul. Whether he knew it or not, he needed her and she'd be damned if she'd die in this jungle now.

'Ready when you are. Tell me what you need.'

Richard suppressed the 'good girl' compliment that sprang to his lips and pulled a fourteen-gauge needle from his pack and one of two sterile empty blood bags.

'Who are we going to bleed?' she asked.

'Me. I'm O neg.'

O negative—the universal donor. It didn't matter what blood type Fumradi was, it was safe to give him O-negative blood.

Richard also knew, as soldiers were screened before going away to places such as these, that he was clean.

He had no communicable or blood-borne diseases that could be passed onto another person. The army did it as a matter of course to ensure they had a known clean source of blood donations at their fingertips within their own forces.

Of course, he could have bled anyone here but not being able to check their blood type, plus the unknown factor of communicable disease, left Richard with little choice. Not that the disease angle was a huge issue for a dying man—Fumradi would be dead before he caught anything from a transfusion of questionable blood.

There was also another angle. If John could see that Richard was willing to give his own blood to save the rebel leader, that might win him some brownie points. Still, he had to weigh that against the fact that a sprint through the jungle would be better accomplished with all his current blood supply. Whatever way he looked at it, the fact remained—a transfusion would buy them valuable time.

The process of taking blood and starting the transfusion into their patient would take about half an hour. He handed Holly the tourniquet, sat on the edge of Fumradi's low bed and held his arm down at his side. She knelt before him on her haunches, and he gritted his teeth as her fingers stroked his skin, trying to find a vein.

She didn't really need to, she thought as a huge vein rose before her eyes from the constrictive pressure of the tourniquet. But contact with him made her feel more assured and…he had very nice arms.

'Just a scratch now,' she murmured, forcing herself to concentrate on the job. She didn't know why she'd said it. Habit?

She slid the large-bore needle into a bulging vein at the crook of his elbow. Richard clenched and unclenched his fist and they watched as his dark blood flowed down the tubing and into the empty bag that sat on the floor, using gravity to their best advantage.

'What are you doing?' asked John, watching them suspiciously.

'He is anaemic. He needs a blood transfusion. I'm giving him some of mine.'

John stared at them both for a while and Holly thought she could see admiration melt some of the ice in John's eyes. Then he laughed and they both looked at him.

'So you will be blood brothers?' And he laughed some more. 'An Australian army medic and his enemy, a rebel leader? Come, now, Sergeant, you must see the irony in that.' Further laughter escaped his thin lips.

'I told you already. I treat everyone who needs my medical expertise the same. Who you are or what you've done doesn't come into it.'

Twenty minutes later Holly was setting up the giving set and hooking the donation up to their patient—talk about fresh blood! She set it to run fairly quickly. The bag was as full as it could get so she figured there was probably five hundred mils in total. It should be complete in an hour which, given Fumradi's demand for fill, wouldn't be too fast.

'We've done all we can for now,' said Richard, turning to John.

'He looks better already,' said John.

Richard had to admit he did, too, but he also knew that the rally would only be temporary. Fumradi was too ill for such simple interventions to have an effect. It was just that after days of having no medical care at all Fumradi was bound to respond to basic fluid resuscitation measures. He had to feel a hell of a lot better.

'What happens now?' asked John.

'The blood transfusion should be finished within the hour. After that we wait. You should know it's not too late to get him to a hospital.'

'Tsk, tsk, tsk.' John smiled. 'You really need to have more faith in your abilities. You can stay with Fumradi,' he said to Richard. 'Holly, would you like to freshen up? I know how you women like to pamper yourselves.'

Holly looked at Richard.

'Where are you taking her?' demanded Richard.

'Relax, Sergeant. Just because we live in a jungle doesn't mean we are without class. Fumradi's house is very well appointed. I am showing Holly to the shower.'

Holly felt her spirits lift. What bliss. A shower? Really?

'She showers alone,' said Richard, a harsh edge to his voice.

Her spirits dropped like a stone. She hadn't even thought of the shower being anything other than her, a cake of soap and running water. She swallowed.

'But of course, Sergeant,' said John, his voice steely. 'I am insulted that you would think otherwise.'

Holly followed John, apprehensive now. She glanced at Richard and he smiled at her to ease her concern. She need not have worried. Aside from the vague creepy smile he gave her, John was as good as his word, showing her to the room next to Fumradi's and telling her this was where they would sleep. It was basic but had low beds and was a vast improvement on hard earth.

Then he took her to a room with a rudimentary shower. He showed her how to pull the lever and she watched as water sprayed out. He pointed to toiletries on a wooden shelf—soap, toothpaste and shampoo—and then left her.

Holly stood still for a moment, quite unable to believe the luxuries before her. And then she stripped. She had her clothes off so fast and was under the spray so quickly her teeth rattled. The water was cooling on her sweaty body and the soap and shampoo, although obviously not bought from an expensive boutique, felt wonderful against her skin and in her hair.

She was standing on an elevated slatted platform and the soapy water ran straight through the slats. Through them she could just see the forest floor beneath. She scrubbed her knick-ers under the shower. OK she was going to have to get back into them wet but it wouldn't be the first time this ordeal that they had been saturated. In fact, they had rarely been dry. At least they were clean and wet!

She wanted to stay longer, stay for ever, under the wonder-ful spray but the urge to return to Richard was stronger. She re-luctantly pulled the lever and the stream cut off. She towelled herself quickly and got back into her clothes.

There was no toothbrush so she used her finger and no hair-brush so she used her fingers again to comb her short tresses into order. Then she noticed a smallish mirror and hesitantly inspected her face in it. Oh, God! She looked a wreck!

She threw the mirror down in disgust. There was absolutely nothing she could do about it now and if they ever got out of this alive and she managed to convince Richard to take a chance, he couldn't say he hadn't seen her at her worst.

Holly made her way to Fumradi's room. She passed a win-dow that had no glass and noticed Tundol lugging heavy wood onto the pile near the fireplace. She was struck again by his so-lemnity. For her, he typified the typhoon crisis. It was about people. People such as little Tundol, who had been left alone to fend for himself.

He looked up and his solemn brown gaze met hers. They stared at each other for a few seconds, both captives in a strange environment, and then she smiled at him and waved. He stood by the fire, unmoving, and then she saw the barest smile touch his lips and he waggled his fingers at her ever so slightly.

Someone yelled for him and he broke contact, dropped the wood and scampered away. Her heart broke for him and she felt her earlier conviction return tenfold. She would not leave this camp without him. If they were going to escape then they had to offer him that chance as well. There could be people out there, looking for him.

She made her way to Fumradi's room and felt her heart pick up in tempo as each step drew her closer. What would she find? She pushed his door open with great trepidation. She stopped in her tracks when she saw him propped up in bed, talking to John.

She glanced at the almost empty blood bag. And then at Richard. He shrugged, plainly as amazed as she was. They had thought he would rally, but this much? True, beneath his illness he looked young and fit, but Holly would never have thought he'd improve this much.

John said something to the local woman who had been tending to Fumradi and she bowed and rushed out of the room, her eyes alight with joy and happiness.

'Our leader has returned to us,' he said to Richard and Holly. 'Tonight we celebrate with a huge feast. You may leave us now. Retire to your quarters. I will speak with you presently.'

Holly and Richard backed out of the room and she showed him where they would sleep next door.

'Did I really just see that?' Holly asked once they were behind closed doors.

'Uh-huh,' confirmed Richard. 'It's only temporary, Holly. It's not going to last. But at least we have a reprieve and some breathing space.' He was trying to be exuberant about it but she smelt fantastic and looked fresh and clean from the shower and he just wanted to crawl into a bed beside her and sleep for ever. The adrenaline surge that had buzzed through his system as he had ministered to Fumradi under John's eagle gaze had left him depleted and washed out.

'I know but…who would have thought he'd have rallied that well?'

'Well, he's got youth on his side. But he's still really weak, don't be fooled.'

A brief knock interrupted their conversation and the door opened.

'You have done well, Sergeant,' said John. 'Fumradi feels much better.'

Richard nodded. 'Good. Then I demand that you let us leave. You gave me your word you would release us when Fumradi was cured. I demand you keep it.'

'It is dark, Sergeant,' said Fumradi, smiling at his captive's audacity. 'If our brave leader continues to be well in the morning then I will keep my word. You will be freed.'

'I don't mind a midnight stroll,' said Richard.

'Be that as it may. Morning will be plenty soon enough. I ask that you remain in your room. I will be staying with him for the next couple of hours. I will let you know when I leave and ask you to check regularly on him after that. I wish to hear immediately if there is a change in his condition.'

John left without a backward glance. They stared at each other for a few seconds. Holly noted how tired Richard looked and guessed donating half a litre of blood hadn't helped.

'We don't have much time,' he said to her, leading her over to the two single beds and sitting on the edge of one. 'We need to talk about escape plans. I don't know how long Fumradi will last.' At least it would keep his mind off how fantastic she smelt.

She sat on the other bed and their knees almost touched across the small distance between them. He ran through everything he could think of about the plan. They would wait until everyone had settled for the night, providing Fumradi lasted that long and leave when the camp was quiet. That would hopefully buy them a few hours before they were discovered to be missing.

'What about Tundol?' she asked.

'If he comes quietly. But if he protests, we're going to have to leave him. We can't afford to have him alert the rest of the camp.'

Holly knew Richard was being sensible. But she also knew her conscience just wouldn't allow her to leave the boy behind.

'He'll come. I know he will,' she said vehemently.

They strategised for the next couple of hours while the noises from the camp outside indicated a celebration was going on. They could hear drums and a beautifully haunting instrument similar to wooden pipes echoing through the camp. Delicious aromas wafted up to meet them. Laughter and sounds of frivolity drifted their way.

She concentrated hard on what Richard was saying. He talked about their journey and the danger areas that the encampments posed and how to avoid them and the effort it would take to get out of this alive. He impressed on her his need for total trust and total obedience, and she swallowed her indignation and nodded her assent.

John came into their room and Holly started guiltily. Not Richard. His face remained impassive. Holly decided never to play poker with him. The man was good.

'Fumradi is tired. He wishes to sleep.'

Holly glanced at Richard. Obviously the rally was starting to wane.

'I trust you to check on him. I am joining the celebrations.'

'Sure,' said Richard. They couldn't make their move until after the celebrations had finished anyway. It would be important to know when Fumradi died. It could be the deciding factor in them leaving earlier.

'We'd better try and rest,' said Richard. 'There's no telling when we'll next get the chance.'

Holly felt her heart hammering in her chest as she reclined on the narrow bed. What they were about to do was dangerous. They could be shot and their chance over very quickly. But she knew she'd rather die running with Richard by her side than sit around and wait for Fumradi to die and be summarily shot.

A little while later a woman entered and brought them a huge pile of food in a couple of wooden bowls. They ate greedily aware that they would need plenty of energy for the night ahead.

Richard and Holly dozed on and off over the next few hours. It wasn't the hardest thing to do, considering their strenuous activity to get to the top camp. Even with a mind racing with what-ifs and the noise from outside, Holly managed to drift off, her tired body overruling her overactive brain.

Richard roused each hour and checked on the rebel leader. After a couple of hours it was fairly evident to him that Fumradi wasn't merely resting but had lapsed into unconsciousness again. He gave him a firm sternal rub and elicited no response. His pulse was weak and thready and his peripheral circulation was non-existent. They were running out of time.

He took some time to study the camp from the open window above Fumradi's bed and planned their escape route while the party continued to rage. The fire was burning brightly and as he scanned the area he noticed Tundol asleep on the ground under one of the treetop dwellings, despite the noise. He lay on an old sack and the only thing Richard could tell that was good about his sleeping spot was its proximity to the fire. Would the boy come with them?

He checked on Fumradi around midnight. The party was all but over. Richard could just see a few stragglers making their way home. They seemed to weave a bit and Richard was cheered by the thought that the whole camp may have indulged in a little too much of whatever alcoholic beverage rebels drank.

He left the window and stood looking down at the rebel leader. Was his chest moving? The door opened. It was John.

'How is he?' he asked.

Richard noticed John's unsteadiness. Dead, I think. 'He's sleeping peacefully,' said Richard, and hoped he sounded convincing.

John nodded. 'Well done, Sergeant. Get some sleep. Tomorrow you will be set free.' John turned and walked unsteadily out.

Richard waited until the door shut and quickly checked Fumradi's pulse. Nothing. He was dead.

He picked up his pack. They had to get out of here. Now.

CHAPTER NINE

HOLLY woke with a start when Richard shook her shoulder.

'What?' she whispered, disorientated.

'Fumradi is dead.'

The fuzziness cleared from Holly's mind immediately. 'Oh.'

'Yes,' he said. 'We have to leave. Are you ready?'

Holly jumped up, her heart starting to race as adrenaline surged through her system in preparation for their flight. She was as ready as she'd ever be.

Richard was fussing with their blankets and she wondered why he was wasting precious time. 'What are you doing?' she whispered.

'Trying to make body-shaped bundles in the beds in case someone checks on us.'

OK. That was smart. She helped him and stood back a couple of minutes later to admire their handiwork. It would do at a quick glance.

'What now?' she asked.

'Follow me. Step where I step. Stop when I tell you. Go when I say go and run when I say run. OK?'

She hesitated, suddenly feeling the enormity of what they were going to do. Would it be OK? He looked at her questioningly. She took a deep breath, nodded decisively and smiled at him. He was with her. Of course it would be OK.

They moved quietly through the silent house. Richard led her to a window he had passed earlier that backed onto the jungle. He indicated he was going out first and she was to follow him.

Being the back of the house, it was also closer to the ground so there wasn't much of a drop. Richard accomplished it easily. Holly threw his pack down to him and then took a deep steadying breath as she prepared to join him.

It wasn't quite as effortless as Richard had made it seem, but she managed to climb out and then let go, falling a short distance into the safety of Richard's arms. She slid down his body until her feet touched the crackly forest floor. She was breathing hard and felt her insides wobble at such intimate contact with him. He stared at her for a few seconds and then let her go.

Richard shook his head to clear the buzz that had fogged it when he had held Holly against him. He really didn't need this now. He needed to concentrate and be aware of everything around him, scanning for danger. They'd never get out of here alive if she was the only thing he was aware of.

He crept silently through the undergrowth and sensed rather than heard Holly following, which was not bad for a novice. He was trained in combat and stealth, techniques drilled into him until they were instinctive. She was obviously following his instructions to the letter.

They moved steadily behind the elevated shelters, sticking to the cover of the tree-line behind the camp. Richard could see the glow of the fire and used it to navigate his way around the camp. His gaze was alert, eyes darting back and forth, and his hearing was tuned in to the sounds of the night.

He heard a large crack and stilled instantly, melting into the night, indicating for Holly to do the same. His heart pounded in his ears. He heard the noise again and realised it was coming from the fireplace. He felt relief flood through him and he breathed again.

Holly tapped him on the shoulder and he turned to her. She

pointed past him and he looked back to what had held her interest, and realised she'd seen Tundol. He hesitated and she looked at him.

'What?' she mouthed.

Richard thought saving Tundol was the only humanitarian thing to do but it could also be a foolish move. What if the orphan didn't co-operate and woke everyone in the camp? What if he'd developed some strange sense of loyalty to the rebels who, even though they had enslaved him, had saved him from the streets? Could they afford to take the risk?

'What?' she mouthed again. Holly sensed Richard's reluctance but she would not leave without Tundol. If Richard thought she was going to turn her back on the defenceless child, he didn't know her at all.

He nodded at her and they continued their creep until they were directly behind the sleeping Tundol. Richard crouched low and indicated that Holly should stay where she was and he would go to the child.

She shook her head at him and pointed to herself. 'I'll do it,' she mouthed. She pointed to his chest and indicated that he should remain.

Richard shook his head firmly. She nodded hers back vigorously. Holly leaned forward until her mouth was pressed to his ear. She tried not to think about how she had kissed him there just last night. 'He'll come with me, Richard. Let me do it,' she whispered.

Her hot breath sent a wave of sensation to his groin. He ignored it and concentrated on the conviction in her voice instead. Even in the reduced light he could see she meant it. Every instinct he possessed told him no.

'Please, Richard, trust me.'

She was so sure about this. Maybe it was time for him to put a little of the faith in her that he had insisted she place in him? He nodded and then held his breath as he watched her creep forward.

Holly reached the sleeping child and shook him gently. Her eyes darted around the camp, alert for any trouble. Tundol opened his eyes and looked directly at her. She quickly pressed her index finger against her lips and placed a gentle hand against his mouth. He nodded at her and she let out the breath she had been holding then took her hand away from his mouth.

Holly pointed to herself and then turned and pointed at Richard. She crooked her finger at him and then held out her hand. And then she waited. She had no doubt by the keen intelligence she had seen in his eyes that he knew what she was asking. Would he come with them in their bid for freedom or would he refuse? And if he refused, would he turn them in?

Richard held another breath. Come on, Tundol. They didn't have all night. He was acutely aware that if the child yelled out, they were screwed. They might have to make a run for it earlier than he'd thought.

Holly's hand remained empty. She smiled at the child and continued to wait. Tundol smiled back and placed his hand hesitantly in hers. Holly gave him a huge grin and pulled gently on his arm. Tundol had the good sense to move quietly with her back to Richard.

So far so good, thought Richard. Stage one accomplished—get the boy. Now for stage two—escape the top camp without detection. Richard knew if they could do that then hopefully they'd almost be at the middle camp by dawn. He was counting on everyone in top camp being too hungover to notice they had gone or to realise their leader was dead.

They continued to skirt the outer perimeter of the camp until they'd almost reached the track that led down the mountain. Holly and Tundol were being impressively quiet. He spotted a sentry almost too late. They were about a metre from him when Richard realised.

It was quite dark. Overhead Richard could see a moon that looked almost full but only speckled light filtered through the canopy above. Luckily for them, although Richard was sure that John wouldn't see it quite the same way, the lookout was sound asleep, snoring softly, propped against a tree. A little too much party cheer?

He led his team a little deeper into the jungle to go around the sentry and then brought them back out onto the track a few hundred metres away from the camp. Richard couldn't help feeling relieved as stage two was completed. Hopefully the next bit would be easier. They simply had to make their way as fast as they could down the track before the sun rose or Fumradi was discovered.

Easy? Not really. If it were just him he'd be really confident of success, but not only did he have Holly in tow, there was also a child. The odds had narrowed considerably. Plus it was dark, which while advantageous on many levels made the trip on a mountain path that was often narrow and littered with swamps that much more treacherous. At least rainfall seemed to occur mainly during daylight hours. Dark he could handle. Slippery could be lethal.

He had a torch in his pack and pulled it out to light their way. He knew he was going to have to conserve the battery, so he switched it off whenever the moon lit their way in areas where the canopy was sparser.

Holly held on to Tundol's hand as they walked quickly down the mountain. She tried not to feel too jubilant. There was still a long way to go, she knew that. But the feeling of release she felt as her legs took her further away from John and the dead rebel leader helped her ignore the protests of her muscles at the cracking pace Richard was setting.

Little Tundol was practically running to keep up and she eased back a little. He didn't seem to be complaining but the last thing they needed was an exhausted child they were going to have to cajole to take every step or, worse, carry. His little hand was holding on to hers for dear life and she felt the enormity of his trust.

Walking through the darkened jungle was eerie. The muted moonlight threw weird shadows all around them and the animal noises that she'd only heard from the safety of their locked and guarded shelters seemed louder and closer. She felt a shudder ripple through her and swallowed. She'd never been overly afraid of the dark, but there was dark and there was this kind of dark.

The noise of the insects and the almost claustrophobic sense of teeming, seething jungle pressing in from all sides was kind of spooky. She held Tundol's hand a little tighter and reminded herself she was with Richard and he needed his escape partner to be mature. To be a woman. And she needed to prove to him that she wasn't a frightened little girl if he was ever going to accept her as an equal.

Still, it was especially unnerving, paddling through the puddles and swamps in the dark. It had been horrible enough in the daylight but the night made it tem times more creepy.

She wanted to call out to Richard to stay with her, but his long-legged stride was purposeful and he didn't need her fears slowing him down. She'd been tested many times during this ordeal and had not faltered. Had Richard noticed? She refused to undo her work when they were on the home stretch.

Having to help Tundol kept her mind off it to a certain degree. He seemed to be a good swimmer, which made the going a lot easier. If he was frightened about what the water held, he never let on. He just followed her uncomplainingly, and Holly thought that if a young kid could be brave then she sure as hell could.

They didn't speak. Richard turned and checked on them frequently but he rarely spoke to them. He had already explained to her that voices, particularly in the middle of nowhere and at night, could carry long distances. She knew that he was maintaining silence for a good reason but she was pretty spooked and could have done with some reassuring chatter. Even an argument would have done.

The first rays of daylight were filtering through the canopy when they heard a noise that put a chill right down her spine. It was a distant wailing noise, like an air-raid warning from an old black-and-white war movie. Except it was just one long loud note.

Richard stopped in his tracks and crouched low. Tundol flinched beside Holly and she felt his grasp tighten. The forest birds she hadn't even been able to see suddenly took flight in a loud mass flapping of wings and she jumped at their noisy departure.

And then the sound of gunfire. Distant gunfire but gunfire nonetheless. Sporadic bursts. Then nothing. Then some more. Had they found Fumradi dead? Or their captives escaped? Or both?

Richard hurried them off the path as more gunfire, closer this time and coming from the direction they were heading, started up. The game was up, their escape had been discovered. OK. Now it had started for real. From now on they really were running for their lives.

Richard guessed the gunfire and the booming noise had been a signal. The top camp was alerting those further down the incline that the prisoners had escaped. It meant they were going to be actively hunted now. People would be aware and on the lookout for them.

They were only about an hour's walk by his estimation to the middle camp. They had no choice now but to lie low, find a good hiding spot and get started again once night fell.

Richard left Holly and Tundol hiding behind a huge fallen log and scouted the area, trying to find them a good place to conceal themselves and avoid detection. He inspected both sides of the track.

To the left the mountain undulated away gradually, with thick forest and many potential places to lie low. To the right the drop was more pronounced, not ninety degrees exactly but definitely sharper and with less vegetation. It was also rockier. There were flatter areas but it looked less hospitable than the other side.

Richard thought carefully. The left side was the easier option. Finding a spot would be simpler and it would be safer terrain to be walking through once night fell and they had to leave their hiding spot and continue.

But it was also the obvious place to find them. Richard had to try to second-guess their hunters. He knew they'd be thinking the same as he was and would probably concentrate most of their search on the left side of the mountain.

So they had to go right. He clambered down the side, trying to hurry but be as surefooted as possible. If he fell, Holly and Tundol would have no one looking out for them. The thought made his search all the more desperate.

Richard found a rocky platform protected by an overhang in a heavily ferned area. The thick vegetation all but concealed it from the track above and, even walking straight past it, it wasn't easy to spot. He'd almost missed it.

Unfortunately, as he feared, he tripped over one of the many rocky obstacles and fell, putting his arm out to break his fall to prevent sliding further down the side of the mountain. A sharp pain ripped through his biceps and he had to bite down to prevent an expletive ricocheting around the jungle. He ripped off his fatigue shirt and noticed the nasty gash spilling out thick red blood.

Damn it! He didn't have time for this! He reached into his pack quickly and pulled out a bandage, quickly wrapping it in place. He would inspect his injury more when they were tucked away and hidden. For now he had to get back to Holly and Tundol.

He scrambled back to where he had left them, ignoring the pain in his arm. Holly looked scared when he lifted away the fern fronds he had cut to conceal their position. He noticed she was sheltering Tundol's body with her own and felt his heartstrings pull hard at her efforts to protect her charge.

'It's OK,' he whispered. 'It's just me.' He was glad when the fear left her face and she loosened her hold on Tundol. 'I've found a spot we can hide until tonight.'

Richard helped the two of them down the treacherous slope to the platform. It was a snug fit and they bunched together, putting the boy between them. Richard was satisfied they were as invisible as he could make them. And he crossed his fingers and hoped for rain.

And it did. Miraculously it rained all day. Torrential monsoon rain so typical of this time of year. Hard and steady, washing away any footprints that could be tracked and no doubt weakening the determination of the rebels. Driving rain made a manhunt hard going.

Not long after they had settled on the platform and just after the rain had started in earnest, Richard heard the distant drone of an engine. He glanced at his companions but they were both asleep. As it came closer, Richard recognised it as a trail bike.

He strained his ears to confirm it. Yes, it was definitely that. He didn't recall seeing one at the top camp but it was certainly coming from that direction. They must be desperate to locate them if they were bringing out a trail bike in such dangerous, slippery conditions.

Richard felt the throb of his injured arm and took the opportunity to inspect it a little closer. The bleeding had effectively stopped but as he pulled at the edges of the gaping wound he knew it should be sutured.

Holly stirred and opened her eyes and caught Richard inspecting his arm.

'Richard,' she gasped, looking at the jagged wound that looked about ten centimetres long. 'What happened?'

'Shh,' he whispered, placing his fingers against his lips. 'It's nothing,' he dismissed.

'Let me look,' she insisted in an angry whisper.

He acquiesced because he thought that at least it would shut her up. He tried not to grimace as her fingers probed the edges.

'It needs stitching,' she hissed.

'Yes, but it won't kill me. It'll wait.'

'Richard,' she whispered, trying not to let her exasperation at his he-man attitude show, 'it should be closed. It could become badly infected in this environment. Not to mention the scarring.'

Richard snorted quietly. Typical of a woman to think of the scar factor. He was a man, for heaven's sake, and a soldier to boot. A scar was nothing. 'Well, unless you're going to suture it there's nothing I can do.'

'What?' she whispered. 'Big tough guy can't suture his own wounds?'

'I have to draw the line somewhere.' He shrugged.

'I'll do it.' The thought of him surviving this terrible incident and then dying of infection a couple of days later was too much to bear. She loved him. She was going to do whatever it took to have all of them alive at the end of this ordeal.

He got the suture holder and the nylon out of his kit and handed it to her silently. What she'd said made sense. Wound closure in this environment was essential. An intact integumentary system was vital in a place teeming with bacteria.

'Local?' she asked.

He shook his head. 'None. We're going to have to do this the hard way.'

Was there any other way for him? 'Oh, Richard…no,' she gasped in a horrified whisper.

'Yes.' He nodded. 'It's OK. It won't hurt for long.'

Holly hesitated and Richard knew she was going to need a push. 'If you don't think you're up to it…'

Holly took the bait, looking at him mutinously. How much more did she have to prove to him? Her hand trembled as she grasped the sharp instrument with the suture holders. She glared at him and instead of cringing as she forced the razor-edged curved needle through his skin she felt almost sadistically satisfied.

He didn't even wince. She stared at him as she looped the nylon around the tips of the stitch holder and pulled it taut. Nothing. No grimacing, no clenching of fists. Not a flicker of pain or a hint of pallor.

The procedure became a match of wills. The rain and the presence of a slumbering Tundol faded from her consciousness. Each drive of the sharp through his skin became more forceful than the last. Damn the man! Did nothing touch him? Was he completely incapable of any emotions? Flinch, damn it!

She met his eye and wanted to scream as he stared calmly back at her. She plunged the needle through again. How could he stoically sit and have such pain inflicted on him and still look like he didn't need anybody? How was she ever going to reach him if she couldn't even get him to react to extreme provocation?

Richard's mouth flattened into a grim line and he gritted his teeth as the needle sliced through his skin. The throb had been bad—Holly's handiwork was worse, bordering on savage. But he knew there was more than a minor procedure happening between them. It was about more than simple suturing. It was about proving to her that he didn't need anything or anyone. That he was tough. That he didn't need to lean on her.

'All done,' she said, as she tied the last stitch in place, still waiting for some kind of reaction. A sigh of relief? The expulsion of a pent-up breath?

He wordlessly handed her a waterproof dressing and she almost missed his breath stuttering into the air between them as she opened the sterile packaging. She glanced at him and realised that it had taken all his self-control to endure her ministrations and was surprised to feel no satisfaction.

'I'm sorry,' she whispered, instantly contrite, as she stuck the bandage in place. Because she was. Did he realise inflicting pain on the man she loved had cost her emotionally? Sure, it'd felt good for a moment when she'd been trying to goad a reaction from him, but in the aftermath her actions had only appalled her.

The gentleness of her fingers made up for the brutality of her suture job, and he almost forgot the throb that pulsed through his biceps. 'It had to be done.' He shrugged.

She looked away. Maybe, but she could have been kinder. Holly turned to tell him as much but he was sitting with his head back against the rock, his eyes closed. His face looked pinched, emphasising the forbidding harshness of his features. Maybe he would sleep. Heaven knew, they both needed it.

He tried. He really did but the throb in his arm made sleep elusive and the intermittent passing of the trail bike kept his senses alert as it travelled back and forth, hunting its prey. On a couple of occasions he also heard voices from the track above him, which made sleep impossible. Luckily no one even came close to their position.

Tundol woke after he'd been asleep for several hours and Richard placed his fingers over his lips. The rain was belting down and he doubted if anyone could hear them, but silence was a good practice for them all to get into. He dug around in his pack and gave Tundol one of the hard biscuits from the rations he carried in his pack.

The boy devoured it and beamed at Richard when he had finished it. Richard had to smother a laugh. The boy had the most engaging smile and Richard could tell that before an environmental disaster had orphaned him, he'd been a happy carefree kid.

Holly woke too and accepted a biscuit after she'd pointed to Richard's arm and he had indicated it was fine. She looked at it dubiously and Tundol nodded at her encouragingly. The biscuit tasted like sawdust, she thought as she slowly gnawed around the edges. Half was about all she could stomach and she gave the rest to Tundol, who hadn't taken his eyes off it once. He did a good impression of the cookie monster without the noise and Holly looked at Richard and shook her head.

The dry biscuit had made her thirsty and she mimed bringing a glass to her mouth. He pulled from his gear a small bowl similar to the one from the sterile packs and after careful surveillance of the area outside their hidey-hole he pushed the bowl beyond the overhang.

He dragged it back in a minute later, overflowing with fresh rainwater. They drank greedily, all of them. At least water wasn't going to be a problem, thought Holly, even if the diet was basic.

The rain didn't let up, which was both good and bad as far as Richard was concerned. There'd be many more water pools and muddy quagmires to traverse, but it had hindered the rebels' search and given the fugitives cover. But it also reduced their visibility and if it continued into the night the going could be quite treacherous, particularly as they made their way toward the bottom camp.

He looked at Holly and watched her bent head as she ran her fingers through Tundol's hair and hummed quietly to him as she snuggled his little body close to hers and rocked gently. She was doing magnificently. They both were. He only hoped that continued.

Richard realised suddenly how much Holly had grown during this experience. She was no longer the carefree spirit she'd been when she'd come to Abeil. This experience had stomped on that very effectively. He took a moment to lament it.

It was the very reason he hadn't wanted her here in the first place. He had always admired her carefree young spirit and had known from experience that places like this tended to trample on people's souls. He had seen her face some harsh truths on this journey and unfortunately learn some stuff about humanity that no one should have to know.

Richard dozed lightly. His eyes were closed but his senses were acutely tuned into the outside world. A voice, a twig snapping, a leaf rustling and he was fully, instantly awake. Alert. Even the lightening of the rain or the dimming of the light roused him immediately.

Darkness descended and Holly was pleased to be moving off when Richard finally indicated he was going to check things out. It was difficult to sit in one spot, so close, and not be able to pass the time by chatting. Silence had never been a strong suit of Holly's and the enforced muteness was frustrating.

Richard came back and they shared a tin of cold spaghetti. The adults gave the lion's share to the boy, knowing that as long as they drank and had something in their bellies they could rely on their bodies to find the energy they would need. Tundol needed it more than they did.

Holly took the little boy's hand once again and squeezed it as they prepared to move off the platform, out of the safety of hiding and into the uncertainty of exposure. He squeezed it back and grinned at her, and Holly was once again cheered by his spirit.

They didn't go back on the track but walked parallel to it along the side of the mountain. Richard had to use his torch a lot and it was slow going, particularly as the rain didn't let up.

But he wanted to get around the middle camp before they tried the track again. In fact, he was pretty sure there would be sentries all along the path so he was going to need to be extra-vigilant. He decided to keep to the rougher side of the path as it would be the least patrolled by the rebels. Let's face it, he thought, you'd have to be crazy to attempt it, especially in the dark!

Richard halted them after they'd been walking for a few hours. His torch told him they had reached the end of the road in this direction. The mountainside dropped away before them.

They were going to have to go back up towards the track, cross over and try the other side.

Richard, Holly and Tundol lay on their stomachs beside the track, concealed by long grass. Richard waited and watched for fifteen minutes before he was satisfied that their was no rebel activity. Even so he crawled across the path on his stomach and made Holly and Tundol follow suit, only rising to his feet once they were back amongst the trees.

The going was much easier on this side, the slope much gentler, and there were more trees to conceal them. But he was having to use his torch more constantly as the rain meant visibility was very poor.

Holly tapped Richard on the shoulder a couple of hours later. Tundol was out on his feet. She had been practically dragging him behind her the last hour or so. They were standing on one of the many narrow tracks that led off the main one. It was a sticky, muddy quagmire.

'We need to rest for a bit,' she shouted over the pouring rain.

'Shh.' He frowned.

Oh, yeah, right. Like anyone could hear them over the racket of nature! Holly was sick of being silent!

'Tundol is exhausted,' she hissed.

'We can't afford to stop,' he hissed back.

'We have to! He can't go on any more. We're going to have to carry him.' The rain slapped into her face and water rivulets ran down her fringe and into her eyes.

'Then we carry him,' he snapped in a loud whisper, 'but we don't stop.'

She glared at him mutinously. The rain ran over his unshaven jaw and droplets of water hung off his long black eyelashes. Even mad as hell and in the pouring rain, there was something about him that just made her want to kiss him. Loving someone who didn't love you back was awful. Loving someone who seemed incapable of loving was hell!

'He's a child,' she hissed at him as she picked up the sleepy boy and cuddled him to her chest. Tundol laid his head against her breast and shut his eyes.

'We can't stop.'

They glared at each other for a few seconds, breathing hard. And then something so totally unexpected happened Holly didn't even have time to scream. The ground beneath her feet subsided, knocking her on her rear, and she was swept down the mountain with a very awake and terrified Tundol clinging to her.

Richard was also caught up in the mini-landslide. It was like a natural waterslide, the well-defined narrow track becoming a shute that barrelled them along at high speed, along with mud and rainwater.

Holly held on to the frightened child for dear life as her butt hit every stone, twig and tree root on the path. She didn't think about the possibility of the ride ending by them plunging over a precipice and falling to their deaths or ploughing at great speed into a tree. She just held on to Tundol and shut her eyes.

To think she had spent money at water parks to give her this exact thrill—never again. After a trip on mother nature's slide she'd be happy if she never saw another in her lifetime.

Her heart thundered and she could feel Tundol's beating a frantic rhythm as well as she held him tight. Leaves slapped at her face and arms, whipping her as she rushed past. Down, down, down they went. She refused to think that this could all end badly after all they'd been through so far. It just wouldn't be right. It wouldn't be fair.

And she'd never told him she loved him, she thought as her life flashed before her. That just wasn't right either. They might be words he didn't want to hear but Holly knew that she was going to tell him whether he liked it or not. She didn't want to take those words unspoken to her grave. She wanted them out so he knew. So he knew that someone in the world loved him.

Then, as suddenly as it started, the ride stopped and she felt herself lifting into the air and then falling, falling. She held Tundol tight and prepared to fall to her death. When she landed on her butt in a muddy swamp she couldn't quite believe her luck.

Richard splashed down beside her a few moments later.

They were all silent for a few moments, reflecting on the ride. The rain continued to sluice over them and they could hear the falling water behind them.

And then Tundol giggled. He sat up and rested back against her bent knees and laughed. They looked at him for a few seconds and then Richard joined him. His deep chuckle gave her goose-bumps and she stared at him in amazement. What happened to being silent?

Tundol chattered away excitedly at them in his own language, giggling intermittently and pointing at them. Now the ride was over and they were alive, he was obviously revelling in the adrenaline rush. Holly laughed too because suddenly she was alive and that was all that mattered. She had lived to tell Richard she loved him.

'Let's rest for a couple of hours,' Richard said, sobering slightly. He figured they were so off track the rebels wouldn't be looking for them here. At first light he'd try to figure out where the hell they were.

Richard located some reasonably dry shelter beneath a big old tree. They took cover under its huge branches, sitting with their backs to the trunk. Tundol lay down on the soft mattress of leaves and Holly and Richard reclined against the trunk so that their bodies were mostly lying flat on the ground but their heads were supported by the trunk.

Holly was too exhausted to say anything. The rush of adrenaline as they had slid down the mountain and the days of hard exertion had really taken their toll. She drifted off to sleep, only to be woken a few minutes later by a stinging sensation on her abdomen.

Half-asleep, she rubbed the spot and the pain intensified. She lifted her shirt up and her hand came into contact with some slimy sort of bug. It took all her willpower not to scream.

'Richard,' she whispered, trying not to sound as frantic as she felt.

'Hmm?'

'There's something crawling on my tummy,' she whispered frantically.

Richard flicked his torch on and shone it on her stomach. Three fat leeches were having a feed. He noticed her lying rigid with her eyes closed and smiled to himself. 'It's just a leech, it won't hurt you,' he murmured.

Holly opened her eyes and looked into his amused face. 'I don't care, Richard. Get it off,' she snarled.

'What is it with you and leeches, Pollyanna?' he teased. 'You seem to attract them somehow.'

Holly couldn't believe he was choosing now to show his sense of humour and his human side. Or that he had even made a reference to that meeting before he had left for Africa and had become a changed man. Not now, Richard, not when she was muddy and soaked through and had a leech feeding off her stomach!

'Richard! Get it off!'

'Them, actually,' he said, 'there's three.'

'Three? Three?' Oh, God! She was covered with leeches! 'Richard! Do something!' She tried to keep her voice low but the desperate note gave it a squeaky quality.

Richard chuckled and shuffled down so he was closer to her abdomen. How many times had he rescued her from creepy-crawlies? He set about removing them.

'Make sure you throw them far way,' she said through gritted teeth. 'I don't want them visiting me again.'

Richard chuckled again and threw the poor creatures a good distance away.

'Ow! I cant believe how much they hurt,' said Holly, inspecting the reddened areas where they had attached themselves to her skin.

'Oh, poor Holly,' he teased. 'Leech magnet.' His head was level with her stomach and he brought his face down and kissed each red area playfully. She had the flattest stomach. She was so petite. He placed a hand against her abdomen and was amazed to see that it nearly spanned her waist.

She placed her hand on his head as he ministered to her wounds to push him away but was mesmerised by the sight of his head against her belly. His salt-and-pepper hair against her white skin. Her hand stilled and his spiky military cut felt good beneath her touch.

Richard wasn't quite sure what possessed him but as he felt her hand in his hair he knew he shouldn't have started it. He glanced up at her and their gazes locked. He felt heat slam into him, white hot. She was so beautiful. If they weren't in this jungle, if she wasn't so young, if he didn't have a million reasons not to…

He pulled her shirt down abruptly and moved back until he was sitting totally upright against the trunk.

'Richard?' she asked quietly, her belly still burning from his gentle kisses.

'Go to sleep Holly.'

She sighed and turned on her side, cuddling into Tundol's body. Great advice, Richard. Now, tell me how.

CHAPTER TEN

RICHARD woke as a glint of sunlight pierced his shut lids. He looked at his watch. Six a.m. The rain had stopped for now. At least his uniform might have a chance to dry out. He looked down at the fabric that covered his body and regarded its muddy, tattered state.

This uniform had always made him proud, made him feel good about himself, that he was making a contribution. If he hadn't been so dog tired and strung out, he knew he'd be ashamed of its dishevelled state.

He glanced at his two companions. Holly was still sleeping on her side, her arm hugging Tundol close. He remembered how he'd kissed her stomach last night and felt the heat kick in again. What was it about this woman? No one had ever got under his skin this much. Not even his fiancée. He'd spent a lifetime protecting it with layers of armour. How had she managed to pierce them?

He shook his head. It didn't matter. Nothing was more important at the moment than getting them back to Abeil safe and sound. Time to stop daydreaming about milky-white, petal-soft skin and how much he had yearned to lay his head against her abdomen and shut his eyes. Reconnaissance. That's what he needed to be doing.

He pushed himself away from the tree and ignored the parts

of him that ached. In fact, he ached just about everywhere so it was an almost impossible task. But with over half of his mission accomplished, he could grin and bear it.

He walked a short distance away, his senses alert. He looked back up the mountain and saw the route they had travelled so unconventionally last night. It had definitely followed the course of a narrow track. He looked beyond the quagmire where they had landed and tracked the pathway further down as it disappeared into the trees.

Where did these side tracks lead to? Were they short cuts to the camps? If they followed this path, would it lead them to the bottom camp or just get them helplessly lost? One thing was for sure—they had to keep heading down if they wanted to get off this mountain.

Richard woke his fellow escapees. Holly regarded him warily, obviously still feeling a little awkward from last night. He wished he could erase what had happened. Go back to the precise moment he'd taken total leave of his senses and take another path. But he couldn't. If she wasn't adult enough to let it be, that was her problem. He was back in control of his body and last night didn't register a blip on his horizon.

'Let's eat and then move out.' He spoke in a low rumble.

Holly felt stiffness in all her joints and she winced as she sat up and leaned back against the tree. Between stiff muscles, a sore back, a bruised butt, leech bites and Richard's kisses, she hurt all over.

'Let me look,' Richard said, when he noticed her grimacing.

She flinched from him as he tried to pull her shirt up at the back and he ignored it. Large surface abrasions all over her back stood out against her pale skin. Some of the areas had obviously bled and dry blood had crusted in some areas. There were the beginnings of several small purplish-black bruises also.

'It's OK,' she said, shrugging him away.

'Your back bore the brunt of the slide,' he said.

'It's OK,' she repeated. Her back was sore but not more than anywhere else. 'Yours must be just as bad,' she commented, remembering he had taken the same trip as her. She went to lift his shirt but he pulled away.

'It's fine,' he said tersely.

Don't touch me. Yeah. He was coming across loud and clear and her heart broke a little. How was she ever going to reach him? How was she ever going to convince him to let her love him?

They ate another sparse breakfast in silence and moved out shortly after. Richard didn't like travelling by day. OK, the canopy muted the light, but they were still going to be more visible than if they had the cover of night. If they could find and then skirt the last camp, he'd pull them up for a rest and continue the rest of the journey in the dark that night.

They followed the track that had collapsed under their feet last night and swept them down the mountain in a torrent of mud and water. Richard crept from tree to tree, trying to keep the track in sight so he could assess their whereabouts. It meandered down through the forest and, as Richard had suspected, led them to the bottom camp.

They could smell the woodsmoke of the communal fire and Richard guessed they were quite near. He went deeper into the forest to avoid detection as they gave the inhabited area a wide berth. But just when they thought they'd passed the dangerous bit, they were proved wrong.

Richard and Holly looked up as they heard a shout behind them. They'd been spotted!

'Follow me. Run,' Richard snapped.

Holly felt adrenaline rush through her system and despite every ache and pain she surged forward, Tundol in tow, keeping Richard's back in sight, mimicking his actions as he ducked and weaved between the trees.

She realised he wasn't running as fast as he could, that he was trying to keep to a slower pace so he wouldn't lose her and she was grateful. She was about as scared now as she had been any time in the last five days, and she knew if anyone could get them out of this, Richard could.

A couple of gunshots reverberated around the forest and she heard bullets whizzing past her ears. OK. Scratch that. Now she was scared. More scared than any time in the period of their captivity.

Richard knew they had to create as much distance between them and their hunters as possible, so he ran hard and expected Holly and Tundol to keep up. He tried not to run blindly. They were going to need to know where they were should they manage to shake their pursuers.

Then he applied a bit of strategy. He could still hear the rebels chasing them but they had dropped back so he decided to slow and backtrack towards the camp and try to outfox them. After all, the rebels wouldn't be expecting that.

Holly and Tundol followed his movements. He could hear her harsh breathing and knew he was asking a lot of them. But this game wasn't over by a long shot, and he'd be damned if he'd just throw in the towel while he had breath left in his body.

Richard could see the shelters of the bottom camp now. He was getting closer. Maybe they should hide around here somewhere until the men pursuing them had run a good distance in the other direction.

Richard looked frantically around for somewhere good to hide, but couldn't find anywhere that would give them the protection they needed. He took a moment to gather his thoughts. His lungs heaved in his chest, dragging in oxygen, out of breath from their sprint through the humid, seething jungle.

And then it came to him. The camp! The perfect place to hide. Right under their enemies' noses! He whispered his idea to Holly and saw shock and doubt flit across her face.

'Trust me,' he whispered.

Holly followed him, with Tundol holding her hand tight. Trust him. But don't touch him. Don't love him. He asked too much of her—didn't he know that?

Richard chose the shelter that backed almost directly onto the jungle. It would be easiest to enter without being seen and would make their exit just as unnoticeable—hopefully. They just needed an hour. One hour to hide somewhere while the rebels searched the jungle. Then they could leave and head in another direction.

He looked in through the slats and it appeared to be empty. They entered quickly and he crossed his fingers that the occupants wouldn't return for a while. He stood by the door while Holly and Tundol sat on the low bed. She opened her mouth to speak to him but he shook his head vehemently and pressed two fingers to his lips. They had to observe total silence!

Holly didn't quite understand his reasoning for bringing them right into the heart of the enemy. She shook herself mentally. Listen to her! The enemy. She was thinking like a soldier now. Like Richard. Whatever had happened to her beliefs about the freedom fighters? Being abducted, that's what. And being confronted with their treatment of Tuti and Tundol.

Whatever Richard's reasoning, she trusted that he knew what he was doing. He was the big tough-guy soldier after all and he had kept them alive thus far. She had freaked at a few leeches. Out of the two of them, she'd have to say he was totally in his element.

And then it struck her. He was. This was what Richard did. This was what he was good at. Standing watch at the door in his less-than-perfect greens, he was every inch the soldier. She remembered his comments about the army being his family and she had to admit he looked right at home. Had he been right all along? Was their no room for her in his family?

She saw Richard freeze suddenly and then heard approaching chatter. She gathered Tundol to her side and pulled him up with her to stand beside Richard and behind the door.

The door opened and Holly shut her eyes. Was this it? The door shut and Holly opened her eyes again at the gasp that left their unwanted visitors' lips. Two sets of eyes stared at her, at them. Two familiar sets of eyes. It was Mila and Kia. The baby Holly had delivered was sleeping at Mila's breast.

Nobody moved for a few seconds. Holly felt sure they all must be able to hear her pounding heart. What was going to happen now? But then Kia smiled at them and Mila grinned and the two women turned to each other and spoke in their language. Holly let out a breath.

Richard let one out, too. The women they had helped a few short days ago were pleased to see them. They seemed safe for the moment but how long would it last? Had saving Mila's baby and probably Mila herself counteracted the loyalty these women felt for the rebel cause and for their menfolk? He doubted it.

Richard heard the trail bike again and they all froze as the bike drove into the central camp area. Mila and Kia talked together again and Mila gave the baby to her mother, who put him in a sling-style apparatus attached to her front and ran out the back into the jungle. Kia smiled at them and nodded.

Richard glanced through the slatted wood and noticed John getting off the bike. A small crowd gathered around him and soon the rebels that had chased them entered the camp, looking despondent and weary.

John yelled at them. He ranted and waved his arms around furiously. He addressed an older man in particular and Holly blinked when he slapped the grey-haired elder across the face. Kia's lips flattened into a slit and her forehead furrowed into a frown. She muttered under her breath.

As they watched the scene, Mila came running towards John and the other men from the jungle behind them. She was flapping her arms excitedly and jabbering away. Richard felt his heart rate slow right down and pound in his chest. His breathing slowed too and he shut his eyes, preparing himself for her betrayal. Had their ministrations meant that little to her? Or was blood truly thicker than water?

He opened his eyes again in time to see John and the other men turned in the opposite direction. Mila was pointing to the opposite side of the path, where they'd been the night before until they'd crossed over and ended up on the waterslide of a lifetime.

She jabbered some more, continuing to point down the other side of the mountain. John interrupted her and appeared to be giving orders. He snapped and pointed the same way Mila had then picked up a long stick and appeared to be drawing in the dirt with it. He was laying a trap.

Ten minutes later the rebel men ran off in the direction Mila had indicated. John got on his bike, turned around and followed his men. Richard breathed and smiled at a beaming Kia who had also been watching. Had Mila just lied to protect them?

Mila entered the shelter with a huge smile, nodding at her mother and at them. It appeared she had. Richard was eager to move out again. There was no telling how long the men would search in the wrong direction. They needed to get as much of a head start as they could.

He picked up his pack. Kia left them and Mila placed a hand on his arm. It appeared she wanted him to wait. Richard agreed but knew he couldn't wait too long.

Kia returned in a moment with a sack and gave it to Holly with a large grin. Holly opened it and the aroma of cooked food hit her square in the face. She thanked the women profusely. At least they could have a decent meal next time they stopped.

Kia indicated that they should follow her. Her grandson slept peacefully in his sling. She exited the shelter first, checked both ways for anyone who could be watching and then motioned them out. Mila waved them goodbye and Holly waved back as they followed the girl's mother back into the jungle.

Richard was humbled and amazed by the lengths to which Kia was going to help them. She'd sheltered them, hidden them, organised a diversion and was now guiding them to safety. Richard knew that the penalty to her would be high if she was caught collaborating with the escapees. And yet she was doing it anyway.

Maybe Holly had a point. Maybe you couldn't paint everyone with the same brush. Maybe they were just people who felt unjustly treated and were fighting for a little equality. Some chose armed rebellion. But not all. And not all approved of the methods of some of the others.

She led them to another side track. 'Abeil,' Kia said, and pointed down the track.

The old woman grabbed his hands and Richard felt humbled by her sincerity, feeling a tightness in his chest at the emotion clouding their goodbyes.

They had crossed each other's paths only briefly but each had had a profound effect on the other. Kia was a proud mountain woman who looked like she'd been around for the duration of the civil war. Yet still she had put politics and years of hate aside to help someone who had helped her.

Tundol and Richard set off down the track, leaving Holly to say her goodbyes.

'Thank you,' said Holly, clutching the older woman's hands and squeezing them tight. She felt all choked up by Kia's courage and generosity.

'Thank…you.' Kia nodded in return, gripping Holly's hands firmly, and Holly saw tears in the old woman's eyes. 'Thank you.'

Holly stroked the babe's head for a brief moment and felt honoured to have helped him into the world. For as long as she lived, she would have a connection with this baby. It seemed bizarre and fitting all at once.

Kia pointed down the track towards Richard's back. 'He good man. Make good father.'

Holy felt tears blur her eyes as she watched Tundol and Richard holding hands. She nodded at the old mountain woman, unable to speak.

'Three boys,' she said, grinning an almost toothless smile and holding up three fingers. 'You and him. Three boys.'

Holly stared at Kia as her words sank in and Kia cackled with laughter at the look on Holly's face. She looked so old and wise that Holly was tempted to believe her. She kissed Kia on the cheek and set off after Richard and Tundol, her mind boggling with Kia's prediction.

With the advantage of better light and the knowledge that their hunters were far away, Holly found their trip down the track less nerve-racking. The urgency hadn't dissipated but the heart-in-your-mouth-stuff had lessened.

Being shot at had been very frightening. Disturbingly it hadn't seemed to overly affect Tundol and she doubted whether Richard had even noticed. It sure as hell had scared her.

They stopped after a few solid hours of walking down the muddy track. Richard found them a secluded spot where they were relatively obscured and they tucked into beautifully smoked ham, unleavened bread and fresh sweet-tasting berries. It was like a banquet compared to the last few days and they ate until every morsel had gone.

Richard decided to not rush over their meal. They had done well to get this far and he knew he had been driving a young child and Holly, who at times didn't look much older than the boy, very hard. He knew how much his body hurt and he was trained and fit.

Holly had to be suffering ten times more than him. The nasty abrasions on her back would be pulling taut as part of the healing process and the salt from the sweat that must be running down her back would be stinging like mad.

Holly enjoyed the leisurely, sumptuous lunch and savoured

every moment. The events of last night, their death-defying slide down the mountainside and the bullets whizzing around her head were never far from her thoughts.

She tried to focus instead on how near they were, how in a few hours they'd be off this godforsaken mountain and she could have a bath and sleep in a proper bed. They were wonderful thoughts but still her mind flashed images of last night on her inward eye.

'What are you thinking about?' Richard asked, fascinated by the range of emotions that flitted across her face as she ate.

Holly jumped. She'd been so engrossed in her own thoughts she'd almost forgotten he was there. She smiled at him, pushing the unsettling images from her mind.

'About a bath. A long, hot, sudsy spa bath with divine smelling salts and aromatherapy oils,' she sighed as the vision floated before her.

He laughed and she joined him. It felt good to be able to talk and laugh and not have to worry that the sound of their voices would betray their position. They were so close to freedom it was such a heady liberating feeling.

Looking at the much more relaxed Richard, she made up her mind that it was now or never. She had decided last night as she had been swept down the mountain that she was going to confess her love whether he liked it or not. But then, with the leeches and plain exhaustion, she'd let it slide.

That morning, as bullets had rained around her, she had nearly met her maker again without having told him her feelings. She didn't want to wait another second. Waste another minute.

She took a deep breath. 'Richard.'

'Yes, Holly,' he said, his head bowed as he helped Tundol with something.

'I want to talk to you. I don't want you to say anything, just listen. OK?'

Richard stopped what he was doing and regarded her seriously. 'Holly—'

'I know you don't want to hear it, Richard—'

'Holly. Not now. OK?'

'Yes, Richard. Now. I've been nearly killed twice in the last twelve hours. I don't want to go another step without getting this off my chest.'

'We're not out of the woods yet,' he said, and then smiled at his own joke.

She ignored him. 'I love you, Richard. I've never stopped loving you. Yes, I know you think I'm too young and naïve and that you don't need me, or anyone for that matter, and that you're happy with your cosy military family of thousands and that I need more life experience and that I should sleep with more men—but you know what? I'm not Tanya. I would never sleep around. And when we were together before, I never understood your commitment to your job. But I do now. I know that the army isn't just what you do but who you are, and I would never ask you to give away something that is obviously dear to you. And it's OK. You're screwed up—I get it. But I can handle it, we can handle it together, Richard. You need someone who's going to love you despite the nightmares in your head and the sadness in your soul, and I'm that woman, Richard.'

Holly didn't stop to draw breath. She ploughed on, wanting, needing to say everything that was in her heart. 'I look at the torment within you and it makes me love you more, because you did something brave to save someone's life when you didn't have to, in fact, when you were forbidden to, and you've suffered emotionally and professionally because of it. But I know when I look at you that you would do it again in the blink of an eye because despite everything, despite your screwed-up childhood and the betrayal of one seriously stupid woman and all the horrible things you've seen as a soldier, you are a decent, kind, humane man. And I love you for it. Please Richard, let me love you.'

Richard stared at her while she unburdened her soul. Her eyes expressed her utter desperation.

'I'm sorry,' she sighed. 'That came out all jumbled and not very articulate. What I'm trying to say is that I understand it won't be easy but that's not a reason to not try.'

Richard stared a bit longer. No one had ever said those things to him. It was the most articulate, emotional speech he'd ever heard. She'd said it with such passion and such conviction he was convinced that she honestly believed what she'd been saying. But the young always thought they were bulletproof and in his experience very few could be persuaded differently. He didn't want to be there when she realised it. Realised that a man with a screwed-up past made terrible partner material.

'Holly…can we talk about this when we're back in Abeil?'

'No. I love you, Richard. Aren't you going to say anything?'

Richard checked his watch. This conversation had to end. They needed to go. 'I told you already, I don't need anyone in my life.'

'Yes, I know, the army is your family. Can't I be part of that? Let me be your family, too.'

Richard heard the note of desperation in her voice and let the fantasy of coming home to Holly each night take hold for a second. It was appealing on levels he didn't want to acknowledge, not least because right now they were as far away from the fantasy as they could be.

He turned away from her and pulled on his pack. 'Come on, Tundol,' said Richard to the boy, who was watching their conversation with interest. 'Time to go.'

Holly watched the boy and the man walk away from her. She saw Tundol squirm his hand into Richard's and she sighed when Richard opened up his hand to the skinny little orphan. He had walked away from her challenge but if he thought that would put her off, he was wrong.

He had just offered a little boy he barely knew a measure of comfort and reassurance and she wiped the tears that spilled from her eyes. Tears of frustration and love and pride. How could one man evoke so many emotions? She gave up trying to find an answer and followed the two males who had come to mean so much in her life.

They marched downwards for another couple of hours. Periodically they could see through the thick foliage of the trees to the flat lowland below and knew they were getting closer and closer to the bottom. Holly could almost taste freedom.

But, as Richard had said, they weren't out of the woods, and just to prove him right, just as her quads were rejoicing in flattish ground, John materialised from the long grass that grew around the bottom of the mountain.

The first Holly knew of it was the yelp of pain that Tundol gave and his hand being ripped from hers. She turned, reacting that split second too late, and John held Tundol firmly in his grasp. Richard's pistol was held at the little boy's temple.

'So…we meet again, Sergeant,' said John with a hostile smile.

'But how?' Holly was confused. How had he known? Everything had happened so fast. She looked at Tundol, brave little Tundol, and outrage filled her as she saw the tears tracking down his face. With all that they'd been through in the last two days, she had never seen him look more afraid.

'I returned to the bottom camp in time to see Kia coming back from further down the track. I had a hunch…'

Holly felt sick. What did that mean for Kia?

The how didn't matter to Richard. 'Let him go, John. He's just a boy. An orphan.'

Holly recognised both steel and contempt in Richard's voice. She couldn't believe this was happening. Not when they were so close to freedom.

'You didn't fulfil your promise, Sergeant. Fumradi is dead. But…you knew that already. And as the new rebel leader, I must hold you accountable.'

So, John had succeeded Fumradi. Interesting. 'I told you we couldn't cure him,' said Richard. Whatever he did, he had to keep John talking. He knew he could take the older man, he just had to get him to release Tundol. 'Besides, it's what you wanted isn't it?'

'What's that, Sergeant?'

Richard saw John's eyes cloud with questions as his irritatingly sure smile slipped a little. Oh, yes, maybe if he made John angry enough, he could get Tundol released. He refused to think about the similarities between the present and the horrific incident he had witnessed in Africa.

Flashes of that day assaulted his inward eye and he knew he had to suppress them and keep focused on the here and now. He had no intention of anyone getting hurt. Not even John— although the urge to wipe the smug smile off his face was strong. But Richard knew he could do that with words.

'Well, that was your plan all along, wasn't it? Once Fumradi was out of the way, you could assume the leadership. It's not fair, is it John, when these young upstarts assume positions of leadership that should belong to us? So, you left a little of the bullet behind...' Richard watched John intently for any sign of weakness, any flinching from his current position. He was poised and ready to pounce at any opening.

'You think I would put ambition before the life of our beloved leader? Really, that is not the way of a freedom fighter.'

Holly watched their dialogue getting more and more furious as it went on. John had to be joking. They were that close! That close to a hot, deep bath. If he thought she was going to let him end it for them now when they were so close, he had another think coming.

And to hold a child, an innocent child, hostage like that. Hadn't he already treated Tundol appallingly enough? To put a gun to his head and use him to manipulate them was unspeakable. She could feel the blood pounding through her head and thrumming through her veins. Her lungs demanded more air and she clenched her fists at her sides.

Never in her life had she wanted to see someone die so badly. She didn't even have time to be shocked by the thought. This despicable human being who had threatened their lives during this ordeal, had locked them up and manacled them, had just stepped over the line. More than that—he was threatening the man she loved and a defenceless child.

She looked at Richard, who was continuing to bargain with John and edge his way closer. Was this how he had felt on that awful day that still fuelled his nightmares? This white-hot impotent rage that was burning in her gut? This fury at how callous and disregarding people could be? As she watched helplessly, Tundol's muted sobs reached out to her, and she wanted John dead more than she wanted anything else in the world.

'Oh, come on, John. You could have had him evacuated to a hospital at any time, yet you didn't. Instead, you abduct us and we walk for three days before we even get to him.'

'Fumradi refused to leave his house. He ordered me to bring you there,' said John, his voice tinged with agitation.

'As you knew he would,' Richard goaded.

'Why, you…' John raised his gun and made to strike Richard across the face.

Yes! That was the right button, Richard thought, and knew he had John now. He caught John's arm easily as it arced downwards and blocked the lightning-quick punch that followed from the other fist. Tundol, free from John's hold, ran back to Holly and Richard began to try to shake the gun loose.

Tundol catapulted himself into Holly and she hugged him close. She could feel his frantic heartbeat against her abdomen and his sobs being muffled in her shirt. Her rage bubbled over as she watched the two men struggle and with Tundol safe in her arms she felt her restraint snap. How dared John hurt Richard? If he was going to mess with the man she loved, he'd better be prepared to take her on, too.

Richard squeezed the older man's wrist hard. He could hear bone crunching and John yelped and let the gun go. It fell to the ground. Now all he had to do was get it himself. He made a dive for it but John, who was no slouch in hand-to-hand combat, dragged Richard back by the feet.

Richard flipped himself over, preparing to launch himself up at John, but was surprised by the force of the man as he threw himself on top of Richard, straddling his chest and landing a punch on Richard's jaw.

His head swum momentarily. John took advantage of his disorientation, punching Richard in the face again. Richard could taste blood in his mouth. John placed his hands around Richard's throat, squeezing hard and pushing down on Richard's windpipe.

Holly watched as John tried to strangle the man she loved. She couldn't just sit by and let it happen. She prised Tundol off her and was about to launch herself at John's back when her eyes fell on Richard's discarded pistol. She didn't hesitate. She walked the short distance, picked it up off the ground, crept up behind John and pressed it to the back of his head.

'Get off him. Now!' Her voice was surprisingly firm. It didn't betray a fragment of her inward quaking. And inside she was seriously quaking. But her fury at John gave her an outward calm and after days of feeling frantic and helpless, the gun suddenly gave her power.

John's hands stilled instantly and he let go, raising his arms in a surrender motion. He rose slowly and Richard scrambled out from beneath him.

'Stay down,' Holly demanded in a voice that would have done a heroine from a horror movie proud.

'Well done, Holly,' said Richard, brushing himself off. 'Give me the gun.'

'No way,' she said through gritted teeth. 'I'm going to make him pay.' And she cocked the gun.

CHAPTER ELEVEN

RICHARD heard a note in Holly's voice that made him believe she was serious. He looked at her, her chest heaving, her eyes fixed on the back of John's head, her arms held out straight, both her hands gripping the pistol. He recognised the look on her face. Hatred and impotence and rage. She was mad as hell and wanted revenge. He knew how that felt. But he also knew how it felt in the hours and days and the months and the years after. And he didn't want her to go through that—ever.

'Holly.'

She didn't answer. She was so focused on the back of John's head he doubted whether she'd even heard him.

'Holly,' he repeated, louder this time, and she glanced at him briefly. 'Don't do this, Holly, you'll never forgive yourself.'

'He kidnapped us, he terrorised us, he enslaved Tundol. He has to pay, Richard. He has to.'

'He will, Holly. But not like this.'

'Why not? Why not like this?' She glanced at him quickly again, licking her dry lips. 'Jungle justice. He would have killed you or me without thinking twice.'

'You do this, and you're no better than him.'

'He just tried to choke you to death,' she said, her eyes be-seeching him. 'He's a rebel soldier. You told me they were desperate and would stop at nothing, Richard. You told me that. Well, I believe you now.'

'No, Holly. All he is at the moment is an unarmed man,' he said, edging forward as he started to see the first signs of doubt creep into her eyes. 'If you do this, you're going to have to live with yourself for the rest of your life. Trust me, killing another person diminishes you as a human being, no matter what the justification. You want to end up like me? So screwed up I can't commit to anyone and a head full of nightmares I can't stop?'

'But if we let him go, he's going to continue to terrorise innocent people. You were right, Richard. A rebel is a rebel is a rebel.'

'Was I, Holly?' he asked, inching forward some more, still holding his hand out for the gun. 'What about Mila? Kia? If I was so right, they would never have helped us. But they did. I was wrong, Holly. You were right. We can't tar everyone with the same brush.'

'OK, maybe not, but we can him,' she said, poking John in the back of the head with the gun. Richard was making sense and her thoughts were confused now. She felt her anger dissipating. Didn't he have to pay for what he'd done to them?

'We can let the justice system deal with John,' Richard cajoled, sensing Holly was wavering. 'His kind of justice doesn't work among decent human beings.'

Holly's heart was still racing and her mouth was as dry as the desert. Was he right? She'd been stretched to the outer limit of what she'd thought she was capable of in the last few days, and she'd been surprised. She never would have thought herself capable of toying with a man's life. She'd never even fired a gun before. But here she was.

'And that's what you are, Holly. You're not this person looking for revenge. You're scared and you've been through a terrible ordeal, but this isn't you. Don't ruin your life. I'm telling you, you'll never get past it.'

Holly looked at Richard. The note of sincerity jarred her out of the hate and anger that had been clouding her vision. She saw the hurt and the pain in the depths of his black eyes that was always there. That he carried around with him every day. He believed what he was saying. She didn't want John's death on her hands. He was right, killing the rebel soldier just brought her to John's level.

She took a pace back and lowered the gun. Richard took two strides and caught her as she sagged, removing the gun from her unprotesting fingers. He pulled her close to his chest and he could feel her body trembling violently.

'I'm so sorry,' she sobbed into his chest. 'I don't know what came over me. I've just felt so powerless and suddenly…I wasn't.' And she sobbed some more.

Richard held her and told her it was OK and that it was over now. He understood about feeling powerless. He had been a powerless child and he had jumped in boots first defending a powerless woman. He understood the despair that powerlessness bred. He rocked her gently and Tundol joined them. He put his arms around Holly, too.

Richard noticed John inching away and he aimed the gun at the man who he despised at this moment more than the soldier he had shot through the heart. Despised him because he was responsible for turning Holly into a vengeful robot instead of the happy, zany, high-spirited person she was. He only hoped the old Holly wouldn't take too long to come back.

'Don't even think about it,' Richard ordered, and John froze.

They stayed there for a while, Richard comforting Holly until she felt better and then securing their prisoner.

'What now?' she asked.

'We're nearly at the bottom. When we get there we'll lie low til nightfall. We'll be easy targets for anyone from the mountain to take a pot shot at us if we go now.'

'What about him?' asked Holly, glancing at John sitting on

the ground a short distance away, his hands tied behind his back. She expected to still feel hatred but she only felt sorrow. Sadness that they lived in a world where the people within it couldn't get along.

'We'll take him with us and see he's brought to justice.' He smiled at her. 'We're nearly home.'

She smiled back and Tundol joined in also. They could see Abeil in the distance and Holly felt happy for the first time in days. Her heart filled with love for this man who had stopped her from doing something she would only have regretted. It seemed like the most natural thing in the world to open her mouth and tell him so, but she hesitated.

'You were right when you said that killing John wasn't me. Do you know how you know that about me?'

He looked at her warily. 'How?'

'Because we're the same, you and I, in lots of ways. You knew that about me because you recognise it in yourself. That beneath all the hurt and crap that's tainted your life you are basically a kind, decent man, Richard Hollingsworth. And that's why I love you.'

Every time she said it the words slammed into him like a sledgehammer to the gut. He refused to entertain such ideas out here. 'Really? You love me and think I'm a decent man, and yet I killed someone.'

'Yes, but you didn't have a choice. You did what you had to do to save an innocent family. I did have a choice. There were no lives in imminent danger, just a choice to make between right and wrong. Thank you for knowing how I was feeling and the words I needed to hear.'

He stared at her for a few seconds. 'Come on,' he said gently, 'let's get this show on the road.' He shrugged his pack on and pulled John to his feet with the ropes that bound his wrists.

It took them just under an hour to finally get off the mountain completely. They came out in a different spot to where they had first been driven, but it didn't matter. Abeil beckoned and in a few hours it would be dark and they could move out across the open plain and walk to their freedom.

Holly's heart soared and she danced a little jig with Tundol. The three of them looked like such a ragtag bunch of escapees. Their clothes were covered in mud and torn in places, and their skin was caked with days' worth of grime. But they were almost free.

Richard secured John to a tree. His mission was nearly complete. Holly joined him back at the treeline and they watched Tundol run around nearby like a crazy thing, like a child instead of a packhorse. He'd been so long up the mountain he was obviously enjoying his freedom.

Tundol saw a butterfly and chased it. He chased it and chased it until Richard called him back, concerned he had gone too far. He was worried there might be snipers on the mountain that could easily pick them off from their elevated vantage point. They had come too far to have tragedy befall them now.

The child obviously didn't hear him or was too engrossed in his game.

'I'll go,' she volunteered. Holly felt a bit like chasing butterflies herself.

She ran off after Tundol and Richard went and checked on John, testing the security of the bonds. John started to laugh and Richard looked at him questioningly. John nodded his head and Richard followed what he was looking at. There was a discarded sign laying on the ground nearby. Richard didn't understand the writing but he did understand the picture—landmines!

The next few moments happened in slow motion when Richard thought about them afterwards. He turned back to where Holly was chasing Tundol and yelled out, 'No-o-o-o.'

He was running out after them at the same time. He was careful to step where she had stepped, but it was too late. The click as Tundol activated a mine sounded so loud to his ears that it reverberated through his head. He saw the explosion in slow motion, too. Tundol being thrown in the air and Holly, who had been two paces behind him, dropping to the ground so suddenly it was as if she'd been cut in two.

He realised the explosion had been small and his mind was already guessing that the device was probably old and malfunctioning. He reached Tundol first. He was screaming in agony. His right foot had been all but blown off. It clung to the rest of his leg at the ankle by a macerated portion of skin. It was bleeding profusely and Richard knew he had to put a tourniquet on it or Tundol would bleed out through his wound.

'Holly,' he yelled. 'Holly.' He whipped off his belt and pulled it tight just below Tundol's knee. It wasn't great but it would have to do until he got his kit.

'I'm fine, Richard,' she said. 'Just see to Tundol.'

He did a quick head-to-toe check-up on the boy but he seemed to have escaped remarkably unscathed everywhere else. He picked the orphan up and carried him over to Holly. In the back of his mind was their exposure to eyes from above and the location of further explosive devices. He had to do a quick treatment and get back under cover.

'Holly,' he said, reaching her side, searching her from head to toe. He noticed she was holding her stomach where a wound was flowing freely with blood.

'I'm OK, I think I just copped a bit of shrapnel. How's Tundol?'

Her voice was small and Richard was alarmed at the amount of blood he could see. 'I think he'll lose his foot but I've put a tourniquet on.' He ripped her shirt right up the middle with brute force and his heart sank at what he saw. She must have copped a flying chunk of metal to create a wound that size. 'I'll get some fluids running when I get my kit.'

'Get it now, Richard,' she urged him. She could hear

Tundol's cries and they were thrusting daggers into her heart. 'And give him something for the pain.'

Richard couldn't remember ever feeling this scared. Not on the many dangerous missions he'd been on. Not confronting a masochistic rebel soldier. Not with his parents. Not in the last few days.

Holly had a critical injury. She needed surgery. There was very little he could do to stem the flow of blood out here when he couldn't even tell where it was coming from. Richard checked Tundol again as he took off his shirt and then his T-shirt beneath. The flow of blood from Tundol's wound had practically stopped.

He shoved his T-shirt on top of her wound and pressed hard. It was the cleanest option he had.

He shook his head. No. No. No. She would survive. He hadn't come this far to lose her now. That just wouldn't be right.

'Holly,' he said, 'I'm going to carry you back to the treeline. You and Tundol. We need to get out of plain view.'

'OK.' She yawned sleepily. 'Just look after Tundol.'

Richard picked up Tundol and plonked him on his back, piggyback style. He scooped Holly up into his arms as gently as he could and cradled her to his chest. She cried out in pain and Richard felt an ache in the centre of his chest like he had never felt before. And then he ran, bolting back to the cover of the trees.

Gunfire from further up the mountain chewed up the ground behind him and Richard ducked lower and weaved a little with his precious cargo, but still kept to the area of ground he knew to be safe. It didn't make him feel any better that his decision to move his patients had been vindicated.

He placed Holly gently on the ground and Tundol sat beside her. He made a snap decision. One or both of them could die without immediate surgical intervention. He felt fear crawl through his gut. He had to summon help.

He grabbed the flares from his pack and stood away from the treeline a little. He let off two red ones and then a green in quick succession. It was his company code for soldier in distress. He knew they'd be seen back at the army hospital and that help would be sent immediately.

Richard didn't have time to watch the display of the flares burning in the afternoon sky. He had to get back to Holly. Both her and Tundol needed fluids.

Richard tore open his pack and grabbed the gear for an IV line. Tundol's wound was still looking good but he knew that the tourniquet could only stay on for so long. He prioritised in his head. IV and fluids for Holly. Then for Tundol.

As he snapped the tourniquet around her arm, he realised he was chanting to himself. Don't die. Don't die. She was too young and had survived the horror of the last few days. It wouldn't be fair for her to die when she was so close to getting that bath.

'Holly, I'm putting in a drip,' he said, and was alarmed at her lack of response. 'Holly,' he yelled, and shook her.

Her eyes fluttered open. He slid the needle in and she protested slightly. He had fluids running into her as fast as possible within two minutes.

He reluctantly left her side to put an IV into Tundol. The boy watched with great interest as Richard slid the needle into him. His pain appeared to have subsided as the tourniquet slowly constricted not only the blood supply but the nerve supply to the foot and leg. It was no doubt quite numb by now. Richard wrapped it in a sterile towel and then bandaged the towel in place.

He smiled at the orphan they had both grown so fond of and the boy smiled back. Tundol pointed to Holly.

'I know, Tundol, she'll be OK. I promise,' he said, ruffling the lad's hair, trying to be positive when inside he was scared out of his mind.

'Holly? Holly,' he said, shaking her, and noticed the coolness of her skin. He checked her pulse. She was quite tachy-cardic. He heard the *wocca, wocca* of distant helicopter blades and felt a surge of relief. He wished he had a radio. He could alert them to his exact position and warn them of the landmines and the two casualties he had with him.

Holly felt wonderfully warm and she could see the most intensely beautiful white light. It was beckoning her and she wanted to go it. It was so inviting and she knew without anyone telling her that beyond the light was a wonderful world where everyone lived in peace and harmony.

She heard Richard's voice float down through the layers of fog. It was OK. She had told him she loved him. She had got it off her chest, so it didn't matter now that she was being called to a different place. She'd go to the light happily, knowing that she had reached out to him and told him the truth.

'Holly, Holly. Wake up. Help is nearly here,' he said, applying a wad of sterile dressings in place of his soaked T-shirt. 'Stay with me, Holly.'

His voice was so demanding, she thought absently as the light came closer. It was OK. She had tried to get him to love her. There was no shame in her failure. She had shared her love, that was the important thing.

Richard was going out of his mind with worry. 'Goddamn it, Holly.' He shook her pale, limp form and felt tears prick at his eyes. 'Don't you dare die on me. I love you, dammit, don't you dare die!'

Richard had suddenly never felt more certain about anything in his life. It was like he was seeing her for the first time, really seeing her. Seeing the woman, not the girl. The woman he loved. She couldn't die now, not when he had finally realised the truth.

She smiled at him then, a serene smile. Her eyes flicked open. The silly man was trying every trick in the book to keep her from the light. 'It's OK, Richard. You don't have to tell me now because I'm dying. It's beautiful here.'

Goddamm it, no! He had been so wrong about her. She had taken everything this ordeal had thrown her. And she hadn't whinged, complained, nagged, thrown a tantrum or broken an ankle. She'd done everything he'd asked of her and she'd done it without question or complaint.

He had rejected her advances because of their age difference and had dismissed her out of hand as a girl, a child. Well, she may be young but she was a woman, not a child. Hadn't she proved it? Hadn't she proved it plenty during this gruelling ordeal? Why had it taken something like this to make him realise?

'No. No.' He shook his head. The sound of the rotors was louder. He could see them now. 'I love you, Holly, with all my heart and soul. I think I always have but I just couldn't admit it to myself. You've got to believe me, my darling.' Richard felt himself choking up. 'Don't leave me. I need you, Holly. I want you to be my family.'

He gathered her up in his arms and held her close, trying to convey the depth of his emotion through his touch alone.

'It's OK, Richard,' she whispered. 'You don't have to pretend.'

'No.' He shook his head and pressed his face into her neck. What could he say to convince her? He knew she was at the brink but he'd read enough near-death stories to know that people could decide to go or to stay. And he wanted her to stay.

And then it came to him. He recited a string of numbers, his face pressed close to hers. He repeated the sequence again and again.

He knows my phone number, she thought absently as she reached her hands out to touch the light. How darling. How sweet. How… He knew her phone number? How come? He'd certainly never rung it. She pulled her hand back to her side and moved towards his voice.

'You know my phone number?' she asked.

'Oh, Holly, I couldn't get the damn thing out of my head,' he cried, seeing her coming back to him. 'I carry it in my wallet. Look.' He let her go and dug his wallet out of his back pocket. He took out the tatty napkin with her writing on it and she opened up her eyes and looked at it.

'You kept it?'

'I tried to throw it out,' he said, his voice husky with emotion.

'Why didn't you?' she asked.

Richard heard her voice getting stronger. 'Because I was in love with you. I just didn't realise it till now. I've always loved you, Holly.'

'Don't cry, Richard,' she whispered, weakly wiping a lone tear tracking down his face with her thumb. 'What's that noise?' She frowned.

Richard could see the markings on two helicopters now. They were almost here. 'The cavalry, darling. The cavalry.'

'Is Tundol OK?' she asked.

Richard sagged against her and kissed her cheek lightly. She was back. Now he had to get her to medical help, a.s.a.p.! He knew he was taking a risk but he had to get out from his safe position and alert the searching helicopters. He hoped the rebels were lousy shots. He ran out from the bushes to wave at the helicopters.

The downdraught from the choppers as they hovered above him almost knocked him over. He indicated for one chopper to send someone down, and within seconds a man was being lowered.

'Sergeant, we've been looking for you,' yelled the soldier over the rotor noise.

'Well, you've found me,' Richard yelled back. 'We're standing in the middle of an old minefield. This area is safe enough for the chopper to land and there seems to be a safe corridor that way.' Richard indicated the pathway back to their hideout. 'I have two casualties, one with a foot practically blown off, the other with major abdo trauma. And there are snipers shooting at us.'

The chopper medic nodded and tugged on the rope and he was winched back up. Richard ran back to his patients and was relieved to see Holly still conscious.

Gunfire burst out from somewhere in the jungle. The rebels were firing at the helicopters now. The Iroquois returned fire, peppering the direction of the sniper with a loud clatter of bullets. The Blackhawk landed soon after while the Iroquois kept up the covering fire from above.

Two soldiers jumped out once the chopper touched down and ran towards Richard. He met them halfway and reluctantly handed over Holly to one and Tundol to the other. They ran back, crouching low, and loaded their patients into the chopper, taking off as soon as everyone was inside.

Richard sat on the floor of the chopper, shaking as reaction finally set in. He noticed as they lifted off and peeled away back in the direction of Abeil that John was still tied to the tree. He had his head turned to protect his face from the force of the churning rotors as they took off. He would send a crew for the new rebel leader later. For the moment they were safe. His mission was complete.

HOLLY and Tundol were rushed to Theatre after their fifteen-minute trip back to the hospital. Richard was debriefed extensively over the following days and relieved of his duties and ordered home early. He sought and was granted permission to stay by Holly's side. She stayed in hospital for a week, the landmine projectile having nicked her mesenteric vein but luckily causing minimal damage to her bowel or other abdominal structures.

Richard was teased mercilessly by his men as he sat day and night beside her, holding her hand and telling her he loved her. He'd been through the scariest experience of his life—nearly losing the woman he loved—and he didn't want to waste any more time.

'I've got a surprise for you,' he said the morning of her discharge. She was to fly home to Australia the next day.

Holly looked into his black eyes and saw his love for her shinning in their depths. She couldn't believe it had taken her nearly dying for the stupid man to realise what she meant to him. She sat up in her bed and closed her eyes. 'Oh, goody! I love surprises.'

Richard grinned at the excitement on her face and was tempted to just kiss her instead. Damn this open bloody-plan design! He beckoned to Tundol, who was waiting outside, and when she opened her eyes, he was sitting on Richard's lap.

'Tundol! I've been asking for you!' she exclaimed, and opened her arms. The little boy threw himself into them and Richard felt more than a little emotional himself as he watched a tear track down her face.

Holly had been so happy when Richard had told her the orphanage had located Tundol's mother, who had been searching for him for three months. They sat and chatted for a while with Tundol, his hair cut short like Richard's, content to sit in Holly's arms and listen to them.

Holly watched Richard walk away with Tundol as he led the boy outside to his waiting mother. She looked at their joined hands and felt her heart contract. He was going to make such a fabulous father.

She smiled at him when he returned.

'You know, Kia told me we were going to have three children,' she said softly.

He looked at her dubiously. Children? What sort of father would he make?

'Three?' He swallowed hard.

Holly saw the doubt and panic in his eyes. She understood that with his background he'd be worried. But she wasn't. She'd seen him with Tundol. She'd seen him with Tuti and with Mila's baby. And the five kiddies form the orphanage who he had made glove balloons for. He was going to be great.

'Three little boys, all like their father,' she confirmed.

'I hadn't thought about kids,' he said.

'Richard, I'm going to treat you so good,' she whispered, 'that making babies with me will be all you can think of.'

He looked into her eyes and the promise that they held gave him an insight into a life he'd never had or even imagined he could have. A life he hadn't even known he wanted. Until now.

She gave him a long, deep, intimate kiss on the mouth to convince him that everything would be OK. The hospital staff and patients whistled and cheered.

'Get a room,' somebody called.

And Richard was just too happy to care that his reputation as a hard-ass soldier was totally shot.

0506/02

MILLS & BOON®

Live the emotion

Tender
romance™

HER OUTBACK PROTECTOR *by Margaret Way*

When Sandra Kingston inherited Moondai cattlestation,
overseer Daniel Carson was ready to support her. Daniel was
strong yet gentle, a heady mix for a young woman who had
been forced to fight her own battles. Having Daniel close by
her side made Sandra feel both protected…and desired.

THE SHEIKH'S SECRET *by Barbara McMahon*

Laura has been swept off her feet by a gorgeous new man!
But Talique is torn. Laura doesn't know his real name, the
past that drives him, even that he is a sheikh! And just as his
plan is about to be revealed he realises that his intentions have
changed: he wants Laura as his bride!

A WOMAN WORTH LOVING *by Jackie Braun*

Audra Conlan has always been flamboyant and wild. Now she
will repent her mistakes, face her estranged family – and evade
men like gorgeous Seth Ridley. But when her past threatens
her new life, can Audra forgive the woman she once was and
embrace the woman she is meant to be?

HER READY-MADE FAMILY *by Jessica Hart*

Morgan Steele is giving up her city career and moving to
the country! When handsome Alistair Brown meets his new
neighbour, he thinks she is a spoilt city girl. As Morgan gets
close to Alistair and his daughters, she realises that what she
has been looking for is right under her nose…

On sale 2nd June 2006

*Available at WHSmith, Tesco, ASDA, Borders, Eason,
Sainsbury's and most bookshops*

www.millsandboon.co.uk

0506/03a

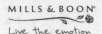

MILLS & BOON®

Live the emotion

_MedicaL
romance™

MATERNAL INSTICT by *Caroline Anderson*

If Eve Spicer was looking for a man, obstetric
consultant Hugh Douglas would be almost perfect.
So kind, so handsome… and so right for her. But Eve
isn't looking! That's what Eve's head is telling her…
Unfortunately, her heart, her body and her every
instinct – do not agree!

The Audley - where romance is the best medicine of all.

THE DOCTOR'S MARRIAGE WISH
by *Meredith Webber*

Doctor Hamish McGregor is about to leave
Crocodile Creek for the job of his dreams. Until
Nurse Kate Winship arrives. She is here to pick
up the pieces of a shattered life and is not ready
to trust again, giving Hamish just three weeks to
persuade her to love him - for a lifetime.

CROCODILE CREEK: 24-HOUR RESCUE
A cutting-edge medical centre.
Fully equipped for saving lives and loves!

THE DOCTOR'S PROPOSAL by *Marion Lennox*

Tragedy has left Dr Kirsty McMahon afraid of love.
She assures herself that the attraction she feels for
gorgeous doctor Jake Cameron can go nowhere.
Until the chemistry between them refuses to be
ignored – and they start to reconsider the rules they
have made for themselves…

Castle at Dolphin Bay
Love and family triumph – against all odds!

On sale 2nd June 2006

www.millsandboon.co.uk

MILLS & BOON®

Live the emotion

_Medical
romance™

0506/03b

THE SURGEON'S PERFECT MATCH

by Alison Roberts

Beautiful and talented registrar Holly Williams needs a kidney transplant, and only one person can help her – paediatric surgeon Ryan Murphy. Ryan is Holly's match in every sense. He has already fallen in love with her and he'll do anything to save her life…if only she will let him.

*24:7 Feel the heat – every hour…every minute…
every heartbeat*

THE CONSULTANT'S HOMECOMING
by Laura Iding

Nurse Abby Monroe is intrigued by consultant Nick Tremayne, and when they work together Abby realises that she is in real danger of losing her heart to this man… Nick has a secret he knows he can't hide forever. But if he tells Abbey, it may mean he loses the woman he loves.

A COUNTRY PRACTICE by Abigail Gordon

GP Fenella Forbes has *not* made a good first impression on dashing doctor Max Hollister – and she is surprised when he offers her a job in his village practice. Soon she finds herself falling for her employer. The question is, having won his respect, can Fenella now win his heart?

On sale 2nd June 2006

*Available at WHSmith, Tesco, ASDA, Borders, Eason,
Sainsbury's and most bookshops*

www.millsandboon.co.uk

066/05

Live the emotion

In June 2006, By Request presents two
collections of three favourite romances by
our bestselling Mills & Boon authors:

Outback Proposals

Outback Mistress by Lindsay Armstrong
Outback Baby by Barbara Hannay
Wedding at Waverley Creek by Jessica Hart

**Make sure you buy these
irresistible stories!**

On sale 2nd June 2006

*Available at WHSmith, Tesco, ASDA, Borders, Eason,
Sainsbury's and most bookshops*
www.millsandboon.co.uk

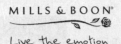

MILLS & BOON®

Live the emotion

086/05

Baby Love

Marriage and Maternity by Gill Sanderson
The Midwife's Secret by Fiona McArthur
The Midwife Bride by Janet Ferguson

Make sure you buy these irresistible stories!

On sale 2nd June 2006

Available at WHSmith, Tesco, ASDA, Borders, Eason, Sainsbury's and most bookshops

www.millsandboon.co.uk

0606/049/MB037

Perfect for the
beach, these
BRAND NEW
sizzling reads
will get your
pulse racing
and the
temperature
rising!

PLAYING GAMES by Dianne Drake
On air she's the sexy, sassy radio shrink – off air she's
mild-mannered Roxy Rose. Both have only one desire –
the sexy handyman next door.

UNDERCOVER WITH THE MOB
by Elizabeth Bevarly
Jack Miller isn't the type you bring home to mum,
which is exactly why Natalie should stay clear of him.
But her attraction to him is undeniable, as is her need
to uncover his story.

WHAT PHOEBE WANTS by Cindi Myers
Men think Phoebe is a pushover, but now she's refusing to take
orders from anyone – especially hunky Jeff Fisher. Because
now it's all about what Phoebe wants.

On sale 2nd June 2006

*Available at WHSmith, Tesco, ASDA, Borders, Eason, Sainsbury's
and all good paperback bookshops*

www.millsandboon.co.uk

0606/108/MB038

Escape to...

19th May 2006

16th June 2006

21st July 2006

18th August 2006

*Available at WH Smith, Tesco, ASDA, Borders, Eason, Sainsbury's
and all good paperback bookshops*

www.millsandboon.co.uk

FREE

4 BOOKS AND A SURPRISE GIFT!

We would like to take this opportunity to thank you for reading this Mills & Boon® book by offering you the chance to take FOUR more specially selected titles from the Medical Romance™ series absolutely FREE! We're also making this offer to introduce you to the benefits of the Reader Service™—

- ★ **FREE home delivery**
- ★ **FREE gifts and competitions**
- ★ **FREE monthly Newsletter**
- ★ **Books available before they're in the shops**
- ★ **Exclusive Reader Service offers**

Accepting these FREE books and gift places you under no obligation to buy; you may cancel at any time, even after receiving your free shipment. Simply complete your details below and return the entire page to the address below. You don't even need a stamp!

YES! Please send me 4 free Medical Romance books and a surprise gift. I understand that unless you hear from me, I will receive 6 superb new titles every month for just £2.80 each, postage and packing free. I am under no obligation to purchase any books and may cancel my subscription at any time. The free books and gift will be mine to keep in any case.

M6ZEE

Ms/Mrs/Miss/Mr..Initials ....
BLOCK CAPITALS PLEASE

Surname ....

Address ....

....

....Postcode ....

Send this whole page to:
The Reader Service, FREEPOST CN81, Croydon, CR9 3WZ

Offer valid in UK only and is not available to current Reader Service™ subscribers to this series. Overseas and Eire please write for details. We reserve the right to refuse an application and applicants must be aged 18 years or over. Only one application per household. Terms and prices subject to change without notice. Offer expires 31st August 2006. As a result of this application, you may receive offers from Harlequin Mills & Boon and other carefully selected companies. If you would prefer not to share in this opportunity please write to The Data Manager at PO Box 676, Richmond, TW9 1WU.

Mills & Boon® is a registered trademark owned by Harlequin Mills & Boon Limited.
Medical Romance™ is being used as a trademark. The Reader Service™ is being used as a trademark.